LAHONTAN VALLEY WAR

A Terrence Corcoran Western

JOHNNY GUNN

Lahontan Valley War
Johnny Gunn

Paperback Edition

Wolfpack Publishing
6032 Wheat Penny Avenue
Las Vegas, NV 89122

Paperback ISBN 978-1-64119-553-9
eBook ISBN 978-1-64119-552-2

Library of Congress Control Number: 2018965401

LAHONTAN VALLEY WAR

CHAPTER ONE

It was one of those glorious spring mornings in central Nevada. That is, one that did not include howling winds, freezing snow, and bitter temperatures. Terrence Corcoran knew that could change in a heartbeat. “It’s mornings like this that makes a man a poet, Mr. Rube.” He was having a one way chat with his horse, riding down out of craggy mountains toward a ranch that doubled as a Pony Express stop several years ago, and was still operating as a stage stop.

“The weather is like a good woman, old man. Changeable at a moment’s notice they are and it is, sir. Warm and lovely, to hateful beast, and back to soft and charming, all in less than five minutes. That’s why we love ‘em,” he chuckled. “Today we ride in sunshine and blue skies.”

He rode as if he didn’t have a care in the world but if one could see, his eyes never stopped sweeping the grand vista before him. He carried a badge and that meant there might be a problem come up at any moment. After all, every man he sent to prison didn't stay there for life. Some got out, and some sought vengeance.

Corcoran's a lawman with his own brand of ethics, won't tolerate anyone mistreating a lady, and a woman is always a lady until she indicates otherwise. He was a deputy sheriff in Virginia City, Nevada, twice. He had to leave the first time because he shot the sheriff while he was in a drunken stupor. He left the second time because he had the sheriff and district attorney arrested for major crimes. He's been a deputy in Eureka County for several years now.

He faced drunken miners, drunken buckaroos, drunken town folk often, bank robbers from time to time, cattle rustlers more often, and highway men too often. "It's nice to get away from all that, Rube. Just you, me, and the great Nevada mountains and valleys.

"I'll have a hot meal cooked by someone else and sleep in a warm bed tonight, my friend. I haven't been to East Gate in sometime. Ralph Carothers was the foreman and stationmaster last time I was through. Oh, can that man tell stories. You'd think he was with old Henry Comstock when they discovered silver in Virginia City, or maybe even with Columbus if you give him enough fire water."

"Course, those boys last night put away their fare share of fire water, eh? Did our singing keep you awake old man?" Corcoran spent more time with his horse than most men do with their wives and used that time to delight himself with bandied conversation. Corcoran was born on the ship that brought his family to New York so had never actually been in Ireland. He's never let that fact get in the way of his being Irish.

He's a big man, tall, strong as an ox, has long wavy deep

red hair, and wears a monster moustache. He prefers hard liquor over beer, smokes long thin cigars, often called cheroots, and carries a Colt high on his waist, a rifle in a scabbard, and if you look closely at his bed roll you'll see a double barrel shotgun tucked away.

He spent the night before along the muddy banks of the Reese River with some friends from the Yomba Indian Reservation. They tried to convince him to ride into Ione with them but he had plans to visit Virginia City, and that was still several days away. Ione was the county seat for Nye County not too long ago, but a nice gold strike in Belmont changed all that.

Ione had some good digs nearby, particularly at Berlin, and a fine old saloon someone named the Ore House. It was, too. Corcoran just came off a three week chase of some nasty bank robbers, still hurt from a gunshot wound to his off leg, and talked his boss, the Eureka County Sheriff, into letting him take some time off. "Well, you haven't had a day off for about a year, so I guess I can get along without ya for a while. Don't disappear on me, Corcoran. Don't make me send out me scouts to find ya." He was laughing as he said that and Corcoran had to duck a feigned left jab that sailed just past his ear.

"I'll be back, Jim. Who else would hire me at such an outrageously high wage? Anyone you want me to say hello to on the way?"

"No, laddy-buck, just stay out of trouble if you can."

Terrence Corcoran had carried a badge for many years, loved nothing better than a good old fashioned knock down drag 'em out the door fight, and woe to the man who treated a woman wrong.

He's spent time buckarooing and mining, riding

messenger on various stage routes, but when he came to Nevada many years ago, he fell in love with the place. The night before he expounded on the virtues of the Silver State to a bunch of Indians who already knew those virtues. "Nevada's like a woman, you know," he was the philosopher under the spell of Kentucky's best. "One minute all warm and gentle and the next a gun-totin' outlaw with death writ large in a sky so vast it's measured in centuries."

He liked to say, "The law needs a little interpretation from time to time. It ain't pounded in stone, just spelled out in ink that can be washed away. Every man has just a tad of larceny in him. It's just that in some it's far more than a tad."

Terrence Corcoran was born on the ship bringing his family to this country from the Emerald Isles, he'll remind you often, and when he finally broke away from the family and came west, he became a true American. "I couldn't abide the east coast and the plains offered nothing, but when I traveled through all these vast mountains from the Rockies through the Great Basin, and into the Sierra Nevada, I couldn't control my heart. Love flowed like hot lava and does to this day."

It was small bunches of cattle along the emigrant road that told the tall man he was coming near the East Gate Stage Stop. The second thing was four quick gunshots. "No, no, Rube. It's none of our business," he said when the horse's ears pricked straight up and he felt the surge of power from the big animal. He kept right on toward East Gate until he heard the cry for help.

"Okay, Rube. Now it's our business. and as he moved off the trail he heard horses clattering through the rocks. "Somebody's in a big hurry. That's a little girl crying. Come on big boy, let's go." He rode down a short draw and up over a ridge in time to see two men on horses moving quickly down the mountainside.

He followed along until he heard sobbing off to the side. It was coming from a stand of cedar bushes and when he rode over to see he found a young Indian girl huddled in the rocks, bleeding from a gash in the side of her head. The pain had to be awful and he jumped off his horse.

"My goodness, little one, what happened to you?" He tied the reins to one of the bushes and stooped down to help the girl. She cowered, crying out, ready to scramble away from this huge man about to attack her. When he spoke to her in his deep soft voice she calmed down quickly.

"What's your name?" She just looked at him. His eyes were soft, warm, and that dark red hair hanging in waves, blowing in the breeze was not a threat. "No habla, eh? Well, let's see if we can get that wound all tidied up. Why are you out here all by yourself and who were those men? Guess you can't tell me much of what I need to know," he chuckled. He had the bleeding stopped and the wound covered and held her in his arms, walking toward Rube. "If I were a guessing a man," he murmured, "I'd say you were about twelve or a little more and you haven't been eating well, either."

What bothered Corcoran most was the wound to the side of the girl's head. "That was made by a bullet or I'm a dead crow. Did those two men chase her down and shoot her? And then just ride off?" He had some bad thoughts rambling around through that full head of red hair and put the horse in a hard trot when he got back on the main trail. The men looked to be white men not Indians, he thought, and they rode off like they knew where they were going. "Why?"

Corcoran rode into the East Gate Station several hours later to find his old friend and get help for the girl. She hadn't spoke a word since he found her and he didn't know if she understood anything he said to her. She was wrapped in Corcoran's bedroll blanket and had her arms wrapped tightly around the big man. He had a hard time stepping from old Rube and a couple of men standing by snickered, watching him.

"Carothers around somewhere?" he asked. "This girl needs some help." The two men lounging on the veranda of the old ranch house pointed toward the barn. Neither man offered a word or any help. Corcoran walked his horse toward the barn noticing a lack of activity around the old place.

"Hope those two gents don't work for Carothers. Sure as hell wouldn't be working for me." He walked into the dark barn, took a quick moment to let his eyes adjust, and tied Rube off to a post. "Wonder where all his people are?"

He spotted Ralph Carothers at the far end of the barn mending some harness and called out. "Ralph, it's Corcoran, Terrence Corcoran. I need some help here."

Carothers jumped up and hurried down the aisle way. "Corcoran! Well, I'll just be damned and boiled in beer. What you got in that bundle?" The elderly man hurried along but was hampered by an old leg injury. Corcoran noticed that the man was also wrapped tightly around his chest.

"Get yourself throwed off another wild horse, old man? Good to see you."

"I am so glad to see you, Terrence Corcoran. There's been some big trouble around here. Let's go up to the house." He was standing in front of Corcoran who was still holding the little girl wrapped in his blanket. "Whatever's in that blanket's still alive, Terrence. You're not pulling some kind of joke here, are ya? Don't gots yourself a bob cat tucked in there, do ya?"

As they walked out of the barn Corcoran pulled a corner of the blanket aside and showed Carothers the little girl's face, tear stained, and half-wrapped in bloody bandages. "My God almighty, Terrence. What happened?"

"Heard some gunshots, saw two men ride off, and found her in the rocks and brush. She don't talk English, in fact, so far, she don't talk. That slash across the side of her head is surely from a bullet, Ralph, that I'm sure of."

The two men on the porch got up and walked off as they approached and Corcoran noticed a frown cross his friend's face. "Those old boys part of the big problems, Ralph? Weren't much helpful when I rode in."

"Those were the Mercer brothers, Hog and Loren, and the answer is yes. If this wasn't a public stage coach station, I wouldn't even let 'em on the property. Let's get her taken care of and I'll tell you all about it."

"Tell me while we're working, old man. I haven't seen you worried up like this, ever."

"It's complicated, Terrence. It will probably lead to Indian trouble. And what's worse we ain't got no law out here. Nye County don't give a damn about us, most of the folks out here don't even know what county we're really in, and the Mercer boys are runnin' things their way. I tangled with Hog last week and ended up with a couple of busted up ribs."

"I see you're still wearin' a badge. You come to help?"

"Nope. Takin' some time to visit old friends like you. Keep on with your tale."

"Cattle that is supposed to go to the Paiutes at Pyramid Lake don't seem to make it there. Young Indian girls have been abducted and violated. At least one has been killed and I think you saved another one today. It's the Indian Agent Joe Hatch along with some mean boys that ride for him along with the Mercer brothers that's created this mess. Indians aren't getting their allotment and the cattle that should go to them is being sold on the open market. There's considerable cattle rustling going on as well."

"Where's the law in all this?" Corcoran asked.

During the whole conversation Carothers and Corcoran were cleaning the young girl's wounds and getting bandages in place. She never took her eyes off the big man and often reached out and held him tight. His eyes and actions told her that, finally, she was safe.

"They ain't no law in these parts, Terrence."

"This is a stage stop, Ralph, where are all your people?"

"I've got a horse man and his wife, a couple of young men out in the corrals, and an old widow lady who doubles as a cook. I run this place mighty close to the wire, Terrence."

"Sounds to me like you're lookin' to retire, old friend."

"A couple more rounds with Hog Mercer and I will either get out this business or be dead. How long you gonna be here?"

"Just tonight is what was in my well thought out plans, but your story and this little girl may have an impact on that."

CHAPTER TWO

"That feller was wearin' a badge, Hog. Was he the one we saw on the trail?" Loren Mercer, in his early twenties, and scrawny thin, was one of the meanest men Ralph Carothers had ever met. His brother, Gary Mercer, known as Hog, partly from his size, partly from his filth, was believed to have killed his parents in order to gain control of the Mercer property in the Lahontan Valley. The two brothers had no use for the law, ranged their cattle wher-ever they wanted, took water from the nearest source whether they had rights or not, did not tolerate rebuke, answered any challenge with their guns and knives.

"I saw that. Let's head back to the ranch. That was probably the girl's body in that blanket. All he saw was our backs, so he ain't after us and she ain't talkin'," he laughed. "She was fun while we had her, though. We'll be back in a couple of days and take this ranch from that old codger, Caruthers. This is good country and should be ours."

Carother's place was at the base of the Desatoya Mountains and there were ranges west of there leading into the Lahontan Valley, generously watered by the Carson River. Some ranching in the mountains, some gold and silver prospecting, but most of the ranching was done in the long valley.

Cattle rustling paid off twice for the Mercer boys. They had a contract with the Nevada Indian Agent to provide cattle to the Paiute Indians. There were several villages but the primary one was at Pyramid Lake. Mercer stole cattle, and the agent bought that cattle, then, according to rumor, only offered some to the Indians. He sold the rest, giving some back to Mercer.

Hog Mercer had put together a small empire in this section of central Nevada, extending from near Watson's Station east through the Lahontan Valley and into the Desatoya Range. That area was arid high desert country with sparse grasses outside the Lahontan Valley. The valley was watered by the Carson River before it disappeared into the Carson Sink.

There were few settlements and many hardscrabble ranches doubled as stage stops and were stops for the Pony Express during its brief life. Organized law enforcement was non-existent. For reasons known only to him, Hog Mercer had an incredible hatred toward all Indians and had caused trouble with the local Paiute tribe often, once almost leading to war before the army stepped in.

The U.S. Army had a small post at Fort Churchill and was in the process of closing it down. There had been two wars with the Pyramid Lake tribe of Paiute Indians over the last few years. In the first war, the Paiutes scored a major victory, overwhelming a force led by Major Ormsby and Captain Storey of the Virginia City Volunteers. The second Paiute war was conducted by the army and they soundly defeated the Indians.

If Hog Mercer had his way, there would be a third war. One of the Paiute leaders, a large man called Crying Wolf had the same feelings in his heart. The Mercer brothers were believed to have abducted Crying Wolf's daughter, raped and beat her to death. Her body was found floating in the Carson Sink. Mercer was never arrested or charged and Crying Wolf had been out for vengeance since.

Carothers and Corcoran were sitting by the fire nursing mugs of hot coffee laced with some brandy Carothers brought in from the Comstock. "That little girl is older than you thought, Terrence. She's skinny as a rail, hasn't been fed much in the last ten days or so, and is probably in her early or mid teens. She has been terribly abused."

"Those men I saw riding off must have been the ones, then. They shot her and dumped the body. Bastards. The last thing my boss said as I was riding off was, 'Don't get in any trouble.' Guess it's too late to think about that. Two white men did this in Paiute country? It's gonna get nasty around here, Mr. Carothers."

"Fort Churchill is empty, Terrence. The army pulled out and turned it over to Randy Watson. He has a stage station on the river across and down stream from the fort. Thinks he's gonna do some farmin'," he snickered. "He and that angry old woman of his took it over a month or so ago."

Carothers spent the next half hour telling Corcoran about the dangerous Mercer brothers. "Those two men you saw on the porch were here to threaten me again. I'm sure that tin badge of yours frightened 'em off. They have run off some good people between here and Fort Churchill. If they see it they think they own it, and God help any Indian that rides into sight."

"Is that where the bad ribs came from?" Corcoran got a nod back. "I don't think I know this Randy Watson you mentioned." Corcoran took a long drink of hot coffee and put his feet up near the fire. "It's been a couple of years since I was through this way."

"Major Randall F. Watson, Jr.," Carothers said with a bit of pomp. "I think that major part was self appointed. He's an arrogant, deceitful character straight out of the northeast. Has no manners and there are some that believe the stock, which he provided the army, was mostly rustled somewhere."

"Is he tied up with these Mercer brothers?"

"There isn't any indication of that. On the other hand there are continuing rumors that some of the cattle that gets sold to the Indian Agency, that don't seem to make it to Pyramid Lake, may also come from Watson." Carothers paused and took a sip of coffee. "His wife Kendra is at least a hundred pounds overweight, ugly as the meanest dog you've ever seen, and chews tobacco by the pound." The two were laughing at what Carothers said when there was a knock on the door.

Corcoran tensed some but Carothers showed no concern as he walked to the door. "Hey, Jaime, come in. Got a little job for you. Terrence, meet Jaime Maldonado, the number one, and only, lawman around here. Jaime, this is my long time amigo Terrence Corcoran."

Corcoran shook hands with a short, heavy Mexican with a long drooping moustache, big brown eyes, and a sombrero wider than the doorway he came through. Corcoran spotted the badge tucked away under the man's leather vest immediately. "Federal Indian Agency Police. Nice timing, amigo."

"Corcoran, eh? I've heard of you," Maldonado said with just the slightest hint of an accent. Corcoran felt immense strength in the offered handshake and knew he was going to like this fellow. The smile was contagious, the gun was protruding from his waistband, and there was a big knife attached to his left boot.

"Maldonado? The last time I heard that name, it was given to a feller riding with Sierra Hernandez in California." He was smiling as he said it but remembered that the Hernandez gang was infamous.

"That was a long time ago, amigo. I'm on the other side now," and he pulled his vest aside to show the badge from the Bureau of Indian Affairs. "There's trouble in this country between white ranchers and the Paiute tribe at Pyramid Lake." He looked over at Carothers. "You said you needed me?"

"We need you," Corcoran said. He told Maldonado about hearing the shots, seeing the two men ride off, and finding the little Indian girl. "She's in the bedroom there. Hasn't said a word since I found her. The bullet grazed her head, she lost a lot of blood, and was cold by the time we got here."

"Jaime speaks good Paiute, Terrence. I'm sure it's little Runs With the Wind, Jaime. If it is, we need to get word to the tribe as soon as possible. Two of Crying Wolf's big boys came by here day before yesterday asking if we had seen her. Let's go see if she's awake?"

"You two sit by the fire and discuss the world's problems and I'll go talk to the girl. If it's Runs With the Wind, she knows me. You said you needed my help, it looks like I might need your help," he said, looking directly at Corcoran. He slipped into the bedroom and the two big men sat down again by the fire.

"You say this Watson is probably a cattle rustler and the Mercer brothers are out to start an Indian war," Corcoran chuckled. "Is there anyone around that slightly obeys the law? Anyone we might count on if all hell breaks loose?"

"Reb Sonnett's a good man. He and his mother run some sheep and cattle about seven miles west of here. Sarah Sonnett lost her husband about ten years ago in an accident that she truly believes was an act of murder. Reb's real name is Aaron, he's twenty one now, about your size or maybe a bit bigger even, and carries a big load of hate for the Mercer boys."

"Thinks they did in his pa?"

"Most of us think that, Terrence, my boy. Just can't seem to prove it."

Maldonado came back into the room, a cloud of anger obvious in his dark face. He plopped down in a big chair near the men. "Don't s'pose you got a drink for this tired old Mexican? That girl told me the worst story I've ever heard. I'm giving no odds that we're in for Paiute War Number Three when she tells it to Crying Wolf."

"Is that your plan? To tell him?"

"My plan is to bring him here to hear it first hand. She's in no shape to be moved, and I want him to understand that all white men are not as evil as the Mercer's. That is, all white men and Mexicans," he chuckled, or maybe there was just a hint of a sneer in there too. "Those men signed their death warrant leaving her alive. I will kill them if Crying Wolf doesn't."

"Not before I have my chance, Jaime," Corcoran almost snarled. "I'll ride to meet this Reb Sonnett in the morning, Ralph. I want to meet this Crying Wolf, too. He's number two out there, I believe, and probably related to old Winnemucca, as well. I have friends in the Northern Paiutes and Western Shoshone, but that won't really matter."

"I'll have a pack ready for you, Terrence. Can I fix one up for you, Jaime. You heading for Pyramid Lake?"

"I am, but I'm all set. I'll sleep in the barn and be gone before first light, Carothers." He looked over at Corcoran, got a little grin on his broad brown face. "I'm riding with Corcoran? That's different," and he laughed loud and strong. So did Terrence Corcoran.

"Ralph, how many we got for supper?" Miss Sadie was an elderly lady, short and thin, but with dancing eyes and a constant smile. "Gotta keep your strength up."

"Just us, Miss Sadie. We'll be there shortly." Sadie Wellesley lost her husband in a terrible stage coach wreck several years before and Ralph offered her the job of station cook. She now has her eyes on being the wife of the station manager. Corcoran had to chuckle watching her cozy up to his old friend.

"Miss Sadie's the best cook on the entire line, from Carson City to Ely, Corcoran. You'll get one fine meal tonight."

Corcoran went to bed with a full stomach and many questions dancing through his shaggy head. *If Mercer was rustling cattle and selling some to the Indian Agent who was shorting the Indians and selling cattle for his own gain, was his agency lawman, Maldonado involved? If the Indian Agent was reselling the stolen cattle, how involved was this Major Watson and why?* There were also humorous thoughts of Ralph Carothers trying to stem off the flirtatious Miss Sadie. Sleep took over after he fought his way through the questions for about the third or fourth time.

A bright spring morning didn't stop the questions and Corcoran had to get answers soon. This Maldonado was the kind of lawman that Corcoran enjoyed being with and he did not want to get wrong answers.

"I've been in this area for less that twenty four hours, Jaime," he said. They were gathered around a large table near the cook stove. Miss Sadie was hovering over Carothers, insisting that she change the bandages holding his ribs in place.

"I've found a young girl who had been abused and shot, heard stories about cattle rustling, and the worst bunch of men riding rough-shod over everyone. One part of that story concerns me.

"I've heard that the Indian Affairs agent for Nevada has been shorting the Paiute tribe its cattle allotment and reselling the animals. You are the law arm of that agency. What the hell's going on?"

"Joe Hatch is the agent, Corcoran, and he's as dirty as they come. Trouble is, I can't prove it yet. Want to do some side work while you're here? I sure could use a man like you."

"Keep going," Corcoran chuckled. "I'm interested."

"Hatch buys stolen beef from Mercer and Watson through a company called Western Traders. Lonesome

Elk, Ed Simpson, called One Eye, and Slim Nestor all work for Hatch and run that company. The stolen beef is sold on the open market to buyers from California."

"You seem to know what you're talking about."

"Yup. Just can't prove it. Yet," he chuckled. "You'll love Nestor. He's a first class bastard from the first word on."

"I do believe I'm workin' for you, Maldonado. You head for Pyramid Lake, I'll head to the Sonnett place." They shook hands, Maldonado insisted that Corcoran be sworn in and told him he didn't have any extra badges so just keep wearing the Eureka County badge.

"Would anyway," Corcoran laughed. "I ain't giving that up for nothin'."

CHAPTER THREE

Corcoran rode north from the East Gate ranch to join the old Pony Express trail west. The country west of the Desatoya Range is deeply cut by gullies and ravines with steep rocky ridges sprinkled about. This made for rough and slow riding. During late summer there were torrential rains with strong runoff and flooding. Finding water in that country wasn't difficult as there were numerous springs, often surrounded by stands of willow and cottonwood trees.

"How do I manage to do things like this, Rube?" Another long conversation with his horse is actually a means of introspection. "A couple of days off to visit old friends and I'm in the middle of an Indian uprising. How long has this Indian Agent been stealing the cattle? How much rustling is going on in this area?" He had to laugh remembering the sheriff's last words. "Try to stay out of trouble."

The Clan Alpine range separates that long rocky valley from what has become known as the Dixie Valley, a lush long valley where the Sonnett ranch had located. The main house sat on a rocky bluff overlooking the wide valley. A spring-fed pond lay on flat ground several hundred yards below the house and was home to a large flock of sheep, all talking at the same time. Corcoran could see bunches of cattle standing off at distances.

He was on a bluff looking out at something special. "Look long and hard, Rube. You don't seen something like this very often. Makes even somebody like me think about giving up this old badge and homesteading in a paradise like this."

Three huge dogs, none of which were the least bit friendly, ran hard to meet Corcoran as he turned to the ranch. Growling and snapping, they didn't bark but the growls spoke volumes about how they planned to protect their flocks. He was relieved to see a rider come out of the dust.

"You're on private property, mister. My dogs will kill on command." The man was probably in his early twenties, carried a big Army Colt in his waistband and held a rifle in his hands. He had dark hair hanging long and tied back, wore a large floppy felt hat, and did not carry a smile.

"I'm looking for a man named Reb Sonnett. Name's Corcoran, Terrence Corcoran," he said. "I'd rather not be dog meat. I come in peace."

"I'm Sonnett. What do you want? You're wearin' a badge of some kind. You should be at the Mercer's, not here." The dogs had been raising hell, racing around Corcoran's horse, snarling, jumping at Corcoran's feet, but not actually grabbing hold or biting. Rube was dancing about some but didn't kick at the dogs. Corcoran had faced angry men looking to kill him on sight, had stood against marauding Indians, fought off some Mexican banditos, but had never quite felt the chill of fear these dogs offered.

"That's exactly what I want to talk to you about. There's gonna be some big trouble around here, I'm afraid. Someplace we can talk where I don't get eaten by these monsters?"

"Let's ride to the house. I'm sure Ma will want to hear what you have to say." There was the slightest move of a hand and the three dogs quieted right down and ran along with the horses, no barking, snapping, or growling. "Don't step down from your horse until I am on the ground and have said something to them or you will be eaten." It was not said with the least bit of humor.

Reb Sonnett was slightly taller than Corcoran and every bit as heavy. He walked with what Terrence called 'an attitude' and led him onto a wide veranda. There were large over-stuffed chairs on the porch, and the view across the valley was magnificent. "I could sit and look at that all day," Corcoran muttered when Reb went into the house to call his mother out.

The valley ran north and south, the large mountains to the east were the Desatoyas, but there were the Clan Alpine ranges between this valley and them, and there were rocky ridges to the west. Grasses, brush, piñon pine and cedar brush stands, and springs surrounded by cottonwood trees were spread out for fifty miles. "If you couldn't raise a herd here, you couldn't raise a herd anywhere," he said, so softly. "Looking at this, almost pastoral, and my mission is to kill the Mercer brothers. This world is a mess."

His thoughts were interrupted when Reb brought

Sarah Sonnett onto the porch. Corcoran jumped to his feet and doffed his sombrero. "Mrs. Sonnett. Hello. I'm Terrence Corcoran."

"Mr. Corcoran, please, sit down. Reb says you're bringing trouble our way." She was almost as fierce looking as her son, and almost as big. She wasn't fat at all, just tall and strong. A ranch widow in every sense of the word. Corcoran could see that before the hardship of running a large cattle and sheep ranch she was probably attractive. Her eyes were full of life and sparkle, but her brows were knit some in worry.

"I'm not bringing it, it's already here, I'm afraid." He spent the next half hour telling the Sonnett's about finding Runs With the Wind, meeting Jaime Maldonado, and what Maldonado and Carothers believed would be taking place very soon.

"I don't have any use for Major Watson or that slob of a wife, but he has as much hate for the Mercer boys as we do," Reb said when Corcoran finished. "I think we need to let him know about all this."

Mrs. Sonnett chuckled just a bit. "You just want the opportunity to see that Sandra Watson."

"Now, Ma, it's more than that, and you know it."

Sandra Watson was fifteen years old, tall, willow thin but filled out where needed, and had Reb's eye. "She has her mother's personality, Reb. You've never spent more than ten minutes with her. Take her out for a three hour buggy ride and picnic and you'll come home with a sour look on that pretty face of yours." She had a twinkle in her eye and smile on her face saying it, but Corcoran got the message even if Reb didn't. "You're a little naive, son. Watson buys stolen stock from Mercer all the time.

Rumor has it that he buys stock from Joe Hatch, the Indian Agent, too."

"I was about to bring that up," Corcoran said. "It seems almost common knowledge, yet I haven't heard of any investigations going on. Someone carrying a badge must be interested in all this. Denying the Indians their allotment, rustling cattle, selling stolen cattle on the open market. Damn. Oh, pardon me, ma'am."

"I've certainly heard it before, Mr. Corcoran, but you're right. There ain't no law in these parts of Nevada. The law ends in Dayton and don't pick up again until you reach Austin. Except for Jaime Maldonado, the Indian Agency policeman, you've got the only badge within a hundred and fifty miles." Corcoran knew his badge meant nothing outside the Eureka County line but figured she probably knew that anyway.

"Other than Major Watson, is there anyone else we should talk to? This is wide-open country and you folks are pretty much alone out here." Corcoran couldn't help shaking his head over what he had ridden into.

"We're alone and like it that way, Mr. Corcoran," Sarah said. "We've made friends with the Indians. I don't think they would attack us, and I'm sure they wouldn't if we help them kill the Mercer boys." She looked at Reb, then to Corcoran. "You go tell Watson what you told us. Me and Reb can take of this place."

"With your guns and those dogs, I think you'll be just fine," Corcoran said. He had a smile on his face as he stood to leave.

"You come eat with us, then ride on, Mr. Corcoran," Sarah Sonnett said, smiling. She walked into the big house, holding the door for Reb and Corcoran. "Got a nice leg of lamb, pot of beans, and fresh bread all ready for us. Man shouldn't ride in God's world on an empty stomach, and our little valley is some of God's best work."

Terrence Corcoran had to smile and agree with that. He wanted to say amen but just couldn't bring himself to do it. "Sure does smell fine from here." It never failed, he thought as they moved into the kitchen. *Whenever I visit a well-run ranch I seem to picture myself being a part of it. Mrs. Sonnett would be a rancher's dream of a wonderful wife and help-mate. It'll never be, I guess, but maybe someday I'll actually settle down.*

"This is a long trail we're on, old man," he said to his horse, "but we'll be at Carothers' place sometime tomorrow. It's been a few years since we've spent time there. Good to be back on the trail," he whispered quietly to his strong ranch gelding.

Pappy Somerset left the Reese River Valley early that morning and was near Carroll Summit as the sun dipped toward its final plunge into the western mountains. "I miss this," he said. He was trailing a pack mule loaded for more than a two-day trek. It took the old army scout less than half an hour to get his animals taken care of, his lean-to up and bedroll spread, and a fire ring filled with dried grass and kindling wood.

"No buff on this ride, dammit, just good old beef. Be better if that was a rabbit on that fire. Oh, well, the coffee's good and hot." He tensed up at what he thought sounded an awful lot like a footstep somewhere behind him. He slowly put the coffee cup down, let his hand roam close to his rifle at his side, and rolled over twice, bringing the rifle up and ready.

"Whoa up there, old man. I didn't mean to frighten you," the man said, standing near a pine tree, a rifle in hand but not threatening or at the ready.

"One more step and you're a dead man. Drop the rifle and the pull that nasty little Remmy out of your pants and let it fall to the ground, and I mean right now."

"Take it easy, old man," the stranger said, but didn't drop the rifle. Instead, he swung it up and never felt the bullet smash through the middle of his head. Pappy jumped up quickly and ran to where the body fell expecting at least one other person to make some kind of play. What he heard was a horse whinny about twenty-five yards down the trail.

"I must be getting' old," he snickered. "Lettin' a man sneak up on me, get that close? Hell, worse than a second lieutenant, I was."

Somerset kept the rifle at the ready and slowly made his way through the trees and brush to find the horse tied to a pine tree. He led the horse to where his was tethered and undressed it. "Man's riding with nothing," he murmured. "Just saddlebags and a slicker. Not ever a bedroll." He walked to the body and rolled it over, taking in a quick breath.

"Sumbitch," he said. "Had drinks with this yahoo at the International Hotel in Austin last night. Gave me that long sad story about being broke and helpless and all. I gave that bastard two bucks and this is what I get back. Well, buster, I'll bury you but I ain't gonna say nice words over your worthless hide."

Pappy had the man under a heavy pile of rocks,

enjoyed the feel of his new rifle, didn't much care for the sidearm and kept it anyway, and rode off early in the morning, trailing a mule and a horse this time. "Should make East Gate by sunset if nothin' else gets in the way."

The trail down the west side of the Desatoya Mountains wasn't as steep as the east side and there were many wide flat meadows on the way down. Great stands of piñon pine dotted the flanks of the meadows. Pappy remembered the Indians of the Great Basin depended on those trees and delicious nuts they provided. "My favorites," he muttered, "were roasted, then mashed into cakes, and dry fried on hot rocks. Cookies," he exclaimed. "Along with mine, they filled many a native's belly most winters." He was in a good mood riding in high rocky country.

Pappy was about three hours out when he spotted a small herd of antelope a quarter mile off the trail. "Ain't buffalo but it beats the hell out of beef," he said. He had the horses tied off and his rifle in hand, making his way down a little rocky slope to the meadow below.

Antelope are intrigued by something moving, a man, a waving hat, a brush moving by something other than the wind, and Pappy took advantage of that. He'd move cautiously through the brush, then stand up, look around, and duck back down. Several of those prong horned beauties actually started walking toward him.

At about fifty yards, he had his sights on a young antelope grazing alongside its mother. "Mine," he whispered, slowly easing his finger onto the trigger. He couldn't see for a couple of seconds because of all the white smoke from his old Hawkins front stuffer, and then saw the herd making for somewhere else. He had that antelope cleaned and skinned and was back with his horses and mule in quick time.

"Won't make East Gate today, boys," he chuckled. "We're gonna make an early camp somewhere, roast us the back strap from this youngster, and have a feast. Let's go find some wild onions to go with it." In his mind there was no finer eating than that on the trail, and no finer place to be than somewhere on the trail.

His days with the army included many of the biggest battles they fought against the plains tribes and his head was filled with memories bad and good. Beans and bacon, roasted buffalo hump or tongue, and prairie chicken too, were his favorite memories.

"Old man Carothers is gonna be happy when I show up with fresh meat." He didn't remember that Ralph Carothers was a cattle rancher and probably had more fresh meat than Pappy had ever thought of.

Corcoran made his way along the banks of the Carson River on the well-travelled emigrant road. He passed through the Lahontan Valley, stopped briefly at Ragtown, and made his way to Watson's Station. It was a typical stage stop with corrals and barns for horses and mules, there were some hangers-on and drifters around the place, giving him the evil eye as he rode up.

A tall thin man with a dark complexion and long black hair watched intently as Corcoran rode in. "Man seems most impressed with my little tin badge, Rube," Corcoran mumbled. "Too young to be a French mountain man and I don't think he's bright enough to be a buckaroo. Sure is interested in us."

Standing off several hundred feet were small homes where coach driver's families lived. Some had small kitchen gardens and more than one was separated from the others by picket fences.

"Wearing a badge seems to bring out the worst in others," he snickered, tying Rube off in front of the run-down and weathered building. A young boy ran up and said he'd take care of the horse for a dollar. "No thanks, sonny, I'll take care of my own horse." The kid muttered something and walked off and Corcoran walked up on the porch and into the station.

"Mr. Watson around?" He asked stepping to a counter filled with trail goods.

A tall, well dressed man in a clean shirt, waistcoat, and wool pants turned with a scowl. "I'm Major Watson," he said. He had a handsome face, wore muttonchops, had bright gray eyes, and flowing dark auburn hair that hung to his shoulders. He put tremendous emphasis on the word Major. "What do you want?"

Impudent and arrogant, Corcoran thought, just as Mrs. Sonnett suggested. He had a hint of a smile taking Watson and his attitude in. "Name's Corcoran, Terrence Corcoran. Like to talk to you about a couple of things happened up at East Gate."

"If you're talking about those missing cattle you've come to the wrong place, mister. You accusing me of something, you just turn around and walk right out of here, and I mean right now." He reached down behind the counter, Corcoran's forty-five was out and cocked before Watson could grab his scattergun.

"Ain't no call for that, Watson. I come to warn you about some possible Indian problems. You want to be a pig headed ass, that's up to you. Now, step back from the counter and I'll be on my way."

Watson straightened up, slowly, backed up two steps, and Corcoran backed his way out the door of the stage-stop. The dark, thin man was standing on the porch but didn't make any kind of move. Corcoran walked slowly to Rube and mounted as Watson came out the front door. "Hold up, Corcoran. Maybe I was a bit hasty there. We've had lots of trouble around here. I'd like to hear about this trouble at East Gate. Don't much care for old Carothers, but if it's Indian trouble, it's all of ours.

"Come in and have a drink with me, tell me what's got you riled."

Corcoran managed to keep a stern look on his face as he stepped down from Rube and retied him at the rack. "I could use a good drink about now," he said. He was surprised when Watson invited the dark, thin man to join them.

"This is Slim Nestor, Corcoran. He's a cattle buyer from the Carson Valley." Corcoran could picture this Slim Nestor as a cattle rustler, maybe, but not a cattle buyer. He remembered hearing the name as working with Hatch and Mercer.

Corcoran nodded to Nestor but didn't offer a hand, which probably wouldn't have been returned. Watson poured whiskey for them and suggested they sit at a table near the stove. "I'll stand," Corcoran said. "A little Indian girl was shot and left to die near the East Gate station. I understand this is the second Paiute girl to have been abducted lately. There is the possibility that there might be trouble coming this way." He drank his whiskey and started again for the door.

"So what if some damn injun girl gets herself killed? Ain't our problem," Nestor said.

"Don't remember saying she was dead," Corcoran said and walked out.

"That's all I know, Crying Wolf. The deputy, Terrence Corcoran, brought little Runs With the Wind into the ranch with a head wound. Somebody shot her. She was also used by whoever held her," he said. He was shaking his head, eyes downcast, remembering what he had seen at the ranch.

"She's being well cared for at the ranch." Jaime Maldonado could see the rage flare up in Crying Wolf's eyes as he spoke, but one thing he had learned over the years was never hold anything back when talking with an Indian.

"You have brought bitter news, Maldonado. We have been searching for the child for seven days. Who did this?"

"Deputy Corcoran said he saw two white men riding off just before he found the girl in the brush. He's not from this country so he wasn't able to say who they were." Maldonado wasn't about to offer any other thoughts on the matter either. It wouldn't take Crying Wolf long to figure out where the problem lay.

"Why didn't you bring her here? You know this is her home." He was angry at everyone and everything, ready to burn and kill.

"Runs With the Wind is badly injured, Crying Wolf. It's a long and hard ride from East Gate and right now she's in good hands." He saw a change in the man's face, from hate to rage. "What are you thinking?"

"It had to be the Mercer brothers, Maldonado, and the white man's law will do nothing about this. They will protect those murdering white men and our women and children will continue to be abused. If any white man tries to protect the Mercer brothers, they will die alongside them."

"I know you don't believe me," Maldonado said, "but there are laws against what they have done, and they will face justice."

"Justice!" Crying Wolf yelled jumping to his feet. "Justice! They have raped our women, stolen our children, killed our men, and they haven't been held accountable one time. Justice? What justice? Indian justice will end this the only way it can be ended. They will die long and terrible deaths at the hands of the women who were abused by them. That is justice."

Crying Wolf turned his back on the Indian Agent lawman and Maldonado knew the interview was over. But it wasn't. The headman turned back. "The white man has stolen our land and promised us food. We are supposed to have cattle provided twice a year, and every time there are less than promised. We can't hunt on our own land and the cattle that are promised aren't given. That's your justice, Maldonado."

The terrible times were just beginning and Maldonado knew he had to get back to the ranches and spread the word. Once started, these angry men might not be satisfied with simply killing the Mercer brothers. There was anger and frustration flowing from years of white abuse. It started with the men hunting beaver pelts along the Humboldt River many years ago.

Maldonado slipped out of the brush-covered wigwam

and mounted his horse for the long ride to the agency headquarters in Carson City. He had been fighting with the current Paiute agent about moving the headquarters to the Pyramid Lake village but Agent Joseph P. Hatch wouldn't hear of it. "My job is to see to it they get their annual payments, not to live with the savages. My God, man, I would never live with them."

"I'll have to ask him about the shortages in those payments," Maldonado murmured. "Everything I've heard must be true and I've not one iota of proof. How is it One Eye Simpson and Slim Nestor are able to get their hands on that beef. Damn me, but I'd love to have to arrest that little rooster."

As he rode from the village he could see Crying Wolf standing outside the wigwam calling to many of the young men. "Hatch won't give a damn about any of this. He'll just shrug it off until the bodies start piling up. The army has pulled out of Fort Churchill, and there is no law in the area. Corcoran carries a badge from another county and I carry a badge no one recognizes. I have cousins in California," he muttered. "Maybe it's time for a visit." He chuckled for a couple of minutes over that knowing there was no way he could just ride off and forget what was about to happen.

"I think you might be right, son. That man Corcoran seemed a steady type but he'll surely need help if Crying Wolf calls for war." Reb and his mother were sitting on the veranda the next morning, talking about the problems that seemed to have been kindled. "Ride to Watson's Station, stay away from the Sandra girl, and tie up with Corcoran.

Don't be getting' all huffy with the major, either. He's just a used up old drunken blow-hard."

"I liked that Corcoran feller," Aaron said. She smiled and thought the same thing, wondering if he might want to learn more about this ranch of hers. *Too damn young for my blood but then again...*

"You keep some of the dogs with you at all times," Reb said. "Ain't that many wolves and coyotes around anymore, so just a dog or two with the sheep and they'll be fine. Keep the others with you." He gave his ma a hug and kiss and jumped onto his big roan.

"Stay well, Reb and hurry home," she said, watching her boy ride off. "He's growed even bigger'n his pa and twice as nice. How come it is I got such a nice boy and old Mrs. Mercer got such pigs? That oldest one, Gary the Hog, killed her and the old man sure as I'm standing here. Reb would never ever have such an ugly thought."

Reb made good time riding to Watson's Station, only stopping for necessaries and one night's camp along the Carson River. The station was busy with two coaches, one eastbound, the other heading west. Horses were kicking up dust, horse boys were moving tired teams one way and fresh ones the other, and the hangers on were getting in the way as much as possible.

He tied off and strode into the busy building filled with wayfarers, coachmen, and others. Watson was behind the counter, his wife Kendra was in the kitchen, and the lovely Sandra was hauling platters of food to the tables. "Mornin' Major," Reb said.

"What do you want, Sonnett?"

"Lookin' for Corcoran, Terrence Corcoran. He about?" If the major wasn't going to be friendly, neither was Reb

Sonnett. Sonnett stood half a head taller than Watson, and was powerfully built. They didn't actually sneer at each other but it was close.

"Probably in the barn. What do you want with him?"

"About the same thing you should want, Major," Reb said. He walked out, didn't nod or say anything to Sandra, and made for the barn. It was chaos as boys and men moved four six hitch teams about, two tired ones, two rarin' to go, and Reb had a hard time finding the big deputy.

"Slim," Watson yelled toward the far corner of the large room. "I'm not sure what the hell's going on but you better get word to Lonesome Elk, One Eye Simpson and Joe Hatch that there's a lawman poking around. Mercer needs to know that girl he kidnapped might be alive."

Nestor's horse was at the hitch out front and he was gone before young Sonnett got to the barns.

"There you are, Corcoran. I see you," Sonnett waved when Corcoran called to him. "Major Watson is in a fine mood this morning. I come with Ma's blessing, Corcoran. We figured you just might need a little help."

"That man in the station's an ass, my young friend. There was another man with Watson. Tall, very dark, and almost skinny. Nasty attitude."

"Sounds like Slim Nestor. Ma thinks he buys the stolen cattle from Hog Mercer and the cattle that don't make it to the Indians. He's a mean one. Carries a revolver and two knives most of the time."

"Yeah, that's him. He was introduced as a cattle buyer but not as a stolen cattle buyer," Corcoran chuckled. "As soon as I can get my horse out of this old mess here, I'm riding back to East Gate. Won't get no help from this fool and Carothers has the little girl. If there's trouble, that's where it will start. Ride with me?"

All Reb said was, "Yup."

They were riding east at a solid miles-eating trot, talking about what might happen. "That fool Watson won't help any of the others in the area," Corcoran said. "He's selfish to a fault, I'm afraid. Can't think past protecting his own and to hell with everyone else. Your mama gonna be okay? Don't much like the idea of leaving her alone like that."

Reb Sonnett had to chuckle. "Crying Wolf will wish he'd gone up against someone else if he tangles with my ma. She's fought lions, wolves, and tough old ranchers all her life, Corcoran. Indians don't scare that woman. You got some kind of plan?"

CHAPTER FOUR

"Well, now, ain't you a sight for sore old eyes. Pappy Somerset of all people to just show up. I'm a sumbitch, Pappy." Carothers threw his arms around his old friend, hugging the man tight. "You still out there in the Monitor Valley?"

"Couldn't drag me out of that country, Ralph. Haven't seen my old friend for years, got to thinking about you, and saddled up. Got room for these old bones for a day or two?"

"You can stay as long as you like, Pappy, but I better take the time to tell you about a little problem we might be facing around these parts. Let's set a spell and talk."

"Looks like you got some sore ribs there, Ralph. You get in a fight with one of those coach horses?"

"No, but they do have something to do with what we need to talk about. Got a couple of real bad boys down in the Lahontan Valley that think they should own everything in sight. Been messing with the Indians, too." They settled in the East Gate ranch house kitchen and Miss Sadie had a pot of boiling coffee ready in short order.

"I got some brandy here if you'd like a taste." She hustled to a cabinet and brought out a bottle. She stood behind Carothers and put a hand on his shoulder, setting the bottle down. Pappy smiled thinking his old friend had himself a woman, finally.

"Gave that up some time ago, Ralph. Just coffee and a bit of sugar, please. You mentioned trouble. What's goin on that's got your attention?"

Carothers stood up from the table with his coffee. "Follow me and I'll show you." They walked down a long hallway and Carothers opened the last door on the right. "That, my old friend, is trouble."

"My gracious me," Pappy exclaimed. "What on earth is a little Indian girl doing at your ranch? Does her tribe know where she is? What happened to her head?" Pappy Somerset had a million questions flowing through his head, and the biggest one was, 'why is she here?'

More than one war was started by way of abducted children, whether it was the Indians doing the kidnapping or the whites doing it, and Pappy could almost smell the tang of gun smoke. "This is trouble spelt large, Ralph. She a Paiute or Western Shoshone?"

"Her name's Runs With the Wind and she's from the Paiute tribe at Pyramid Lake. She's been missing for several days."

They walked back to the kitchen and Carothers refilled their cups, adding some brandy to his. "Another friend of mine, from up Eureka way, was heading in for a visit when he found her along the trail. He heard gunshots, saw two white men ride off, and found the girl. One bullet had grazed her head."

"The two that rode off must have thought they killed her. He brought her here. Do you know Jaime Maldonado, the Indian agent's lawman?" Pappy shook his head. "Well, anyway, Maldonado is at Pyramid Lake now talking to the tribe. Crying Wolf is one of the headman and he's gonna be in a rage when he finds out. This girl is related to him and his daughter was killed by abductors not too long ago."

"Sounds like maybe I got here at the right time. You got any plans, cuz those savages are gonna swoop down on this place some time real soon. Who's here besides the two of us?"

"Right now, it's us, my friend, ready to take part in Paiute War Number Three." They laughed, raised their cups, and drank the coffee down. "Ain't nobody else. My horseman wouldn't be much of a fighter, and there's Miss Sadie. Unless Terrence comes back, it's just us. If he's smart, he'll just ride on into the dust of tomorrow."

"Terrence?" Pappy walked to the stove for the coffee pot. "I rode with a man named Terrence not too long ago. Wouldn't be Terrence Corcoran would it?"

"By damn, it would," Ralph Carothers said, slapping his hand on the table. "You rode with Corcoran? That must have been something. He never tells his own stories but I've heard some real poppers from others. What's your story?"

"We chased down a gang of murderers, kidnappers, bank robbers. You heard of Humboldt Charley's gang? It was them. Corcoran coming back here?"

"I hope so." Ralph Carothers sat quiet for a minute

wondering just what was going to happen. "There aren't very many of us around these parts, and some aren't what might be called good citizens, Pappy. It may have been Hog Mercer and his brother that Corcoran saw riding off."

"We don't know for sure though. It wouldn't be right to suggest that they were responsible if Crying Wolf should ask."

Pappy Somerset got a slight smile out of that. "Yup, might not be right," he chuckled. "Tell me about this Hog Mercer."

"The story is he killed his parents in order to take over the ranch. Ain't no law in this country so don't know if that's a fact. He and Loren seem to not believe in the concept of law and order. Land and cattle are for the taking, water, life, property, too. Just about as bad a family as I've ever heard of."

"To kidnap a young Indian girl, rape and ravage her, and then shoot her in the head and ride off is the most terrible thing I've heard that men could do." Pappy was shaking his head trying to imagine men living like the ancient savages in some jungle somewhere. "I've fought a lot of Indians, Ralph. Killed many, I guess, but I can also say that I have Indian friends, good people, who love their families deeply. Doing something like this to a young girl would bring every man in the family to a rage."

"There's more," Carothers said. "As I said, this isn't the first Paiute girl to be kidnapped. Another girl disappeared, Crying Wolf's daughter, and her body was found sometime later. Many, Crying Wolf among them, believe Hog Mercer was responsible but there was never any kind of evidence to prove it."

"Now, Runs With the Wind will be able to identify the

men responsible. That is if Crying Wolf doesn't just kill everyone in this section of Nevada. He has the ear of the headmen at Pyramid Lake. Crying Wolf will be out for vengeance."

"The only elders I've ever known were Dancing Pines and a feller called Shaking Rocks. Dancing Pines is one wise old man, Carothers. God help us if the army finds out about all this." Pappy Somerset had scouted for many years for the army and understood their reaction most of the time was attack and ask questions later.

The men moved about the ranch house talking about the problem for at least another two hours and were interrupted by the sound of a horse coming into the old stage stop. "Hope this is good news, Pappy."

"Your mother said she thought you folks were in good stead with the Indians, Reb. What about some of the other ranchers in the area? I know about the Mercers, but none of the others."

It was a long two day ride from Watson's Station to East Gate, even pushing it, and Corcoran knew the Indians would come in force if they thought the white ranchers were responsible for the little girl's injuries. "We might not have much time to gather a force to meet the Paiutes."

"There wouldn't be much of a force even if everyone came to help," Reb Sonnett said. "There's old Josh Whitney and his two sons. Whitney's almost as mean spirited as Watson and those boys of his are worse. Bart and Sam are believed to run with Loren Mercer on cattle rustling ventures. The Whitney ranch and range bumps up to the Mercer place."

"In my opinion, Whitney would join up with Hog Mercer and use an Indian uprising as an opportunity to steal cattle, sheep, and land. They would defend themselves, but no one else."

"Sounds like you have some wonderful neighbors, Reb. Anyone that we might be able to count on?"

"Abe Johnson took over the Frankmore property last year when Asa died. He was their foreman and Asa willed it to him. Johnson's a good man, has had problems with the Mercers and the Whitney's. I think we could count on Abe to help if it comes to that."

"What seems to be missing out in this country is families, Reb." Corcoran deputied in several Nevada counties over the years and knew most ranches were run by families. "Seems you and your ma are the closest to a family operation in the valley."

"The answer to that is Hog Mercer. He's run off the small family operations. Ma is sure he killed my pa, most are willing to believe the Kendall family left because Mercer rustled their stock and burned them out. There were a couple of others who left under bad circumstances. Mercer now owns those properties."

"This is way out of my jurisdiction but since I'm the only lawman around I guess I'll just have to do my duty," Corcoran laughed. "Mr. Hog Mercer ain't gonna appreciate me being around, Reb. Count on it."

Corcoran rode in silence, letting his mind absorb all the unpleasant thoughts. He saw a large area of Nevada, settled and sadly, not as economically stable as frontier life could be, no family operations but one, but with no visible law, nothing the settlers could call on for help. The high desert of the Great Basin will support cattle and sheep ranching but it takes a lot of acreage per animal, which means sparse human population.

"What about the coach runs through this country? Watson Station, East Gate Station, and Carroll Summit are all populated. Are the coaches stopped and robbed?"

"Several have been and most of us believe the Mercer boys and Whitney boys are responsible. Again, no help from any of the county people."

He saw many hundreds of square miles with no protection from the marauding Indians or cattle rustling murderers. Corcoran saw an angry Indian tribe seeking vengeance on a small group of settlers spread over hundreds of square miles. Watson and Carothers had both told him that the army was gone from Fort Churchill, so these few ranchers would be on their own. Three or four stage stops connected Dayton to Austin, and not one lawman available to protect them.

"There aren't enough people in these valleys to tangle with Crying Wolf, Reb. We're gonna have to fight this one a different way."

"What would that be, Corcoran? A different way?"

"Major Watson won't join anything we might put together for defense, the Whitney family and Mercer family should be the Indian's prime targets but might not be right at the first, and that don't leave us much. I have an idea that might work and I need to get us all together to talk it out."

"Can you ride to Abe Johnson and tell him what's going on and persuade him to come to the East Gate ranch? Hurry, Reb. We might not have much time."

Reb Sonnett wanted to know more but also understood that Crying Wolf might already be on his way. He nodded, spurred his horse and rode off cross-country toward the old Frankmore ranch. Corcoran nudged Rube into a fast trot hoping to reach East Gate early the next day.

Maldonado rode into Carson City two days after his meeting with Crying Wolf only to discover the Nevada Indian Agent, Joseph Hatch, had left for Washington. There was no one he could turn to for help. A visit to the state's attorney general got him nowhere, the area between Pyramid Lake, the old Fort Churchill, and Carroll Summit was spread over three counties, two of which were not fully organized. There was no law agency he could go to for help.

He made one more stop before he knew he had to leave for East Gate. Major James McPherson was the Pacific Army commander in Nevada, and worked closely with the Nevada First Volunteers, which had two companies in northern Nevada. "Everything we've talked about, Major, is about to come down on our heads. Joe Hatch is in Washington."

"Have you been able to get anything more on the cattle rustling and selling? Those are government steers being stolen. I'm still sure Hatch is involved."

"I am too, Jaime, but without evidence, proof, the army can't help you. Your own agency isn't going to like whatever you come up with. You need proof written in stone, my friend, before those Washington idiots will believe you."

"Or a third Paiute war," Maldonado shrugged. "Another Paiute girl was abducted. This one was shot and left in the brush. She's lucky, though, Major. A Eureka County Deputy was in the area and found her. She's recuperating now at East Gate Station. I'll try to keep you posted. Word of all this has been sent to Fort McDermitt."

"I heard rumors about this, Jaime. I'll alert the volunteer companies. Try to keep a lid on things. Damn that Hatch. He steals their food and Hog Mercer steals their young women. I'd sure as hell want to start a war."

In frustration, Jaime Maldonado packed up and rode as fast as he dared to

East Gate, planning on a quick visit at Watson's Station to warn the Major of the possible raids. The long ride along the Carson River should have been a pleasant experience. It wasn't.

It was a busy road with traffic coming and going from Virginia City, Dayton, and points east. Great mills had been erected on the stretch of river from Dayton to Carson City, which increased heavy traffic even more. The ride from Dayton to Watson's Station was the most pleasant once past all the activity around Sutro City. Great stands of cottonwood lined the riverbanks, grass was good, and there was considerable game to see. Maldonado only saw the threat of war.

History has a way of repeating itself, the agency policeman thought, making good time on a breezy day. The first Paiute Indian War, not long after silver was discovered in what is now Virginia City, was caused by ranchers abusing young Indian girls. "We sure have learned our lesson," he snickered.

"You got no jurisdiction here, Maldonado. Go on about

your business somewhere else." Major Randall Watson didn't wait for Maldonado to even say hello when the Indian Agent lawman walked into the stage stop. "I got no time for Mexicans, Indians, or anyone attached to them. Go on, get out."

Maldonado had heard Watson's rants before and shrugged the personal abuse off, but wanted to just shoot the fool. "There's trouble comin' Mr. Watson," he said. "That's all I came to say. Might want to send your women-folk to Carson City." He turned and walked out, leaving the door open.

"One very stupid man," he muttered, stepping onto his horse. "No more stops now, partner, till we reach East Gate," and he touched his spurs to the horses flanks. He knew he couldn't make the ride in one day, but said it to himself anyway. "Crying Wolf knows that Runs With the Wind is with Ralph Carothers and knows she's being well taken care of. I gotta try to think like he would."

It was a long ride through the Lahontan Valley, around rocky Grimes Point, and he made camp at an abandoned Pony Express stop near a huge sand dune. "I'll make East Gate tomorrow," he muttered, getting a good fire going. If Crying Wolf knows that Runs With the Wind is safe, where would he strike? The Mercers' place is my bet, and for good reason."

Crying Wolf already believed that Hog Mercer was responsible for one Paiute girl's death and he told Maldonado that he wanted Hog and his brother dead. "The big problem is going to be containing the youngsters who will ride with Crying Wolf. They will be riding for blood and will the deaths of Hog and Loren be enough? Will they then strike out and hit one ranch after another?"

It was a fitful sleep and Jaime Maldonado was up well before sunrise and on the trail for East Gate. "I hope that feller Corcoran is still there. I'll need a man like him to stop this. How many ranches are there?" he wondered, driving his pony hard through rocky country. "The Sonnett widow and her son Reb live down in that valley to the north, he murmured. "She's been very helpful to the tribe more than once. For the time being, they should be safe."

He dropped down into a long flat valley, could see the Desatoya Range and knew he was just a few hours from East Gate. "Crying Wolf would spend a day or two working his braves into the same rage he was already in. They would dance to the drums, would seek council with elders and wise men, and then Crying Wolf would turn them loose."

He saw smoke from the East Gate ranch house chimney and knew he was in time, as he rode the long trail into the property. He noticed a couple of strange horses and a mule tied off at the rack as he stepped off his horse to tie it off. "More visitors," he mumbled. "I hope they have guns."

CHAPTER FIVE

Abe Johnson was about the same age as Reb Sonnett but was built like a logger in the high north country; wide, broad, and thick. His body, shoulders, neck, and legs were thick with muscles and many described the young man as incredibly strong. He had long, intensely black hair that he tied back, very dark eyes, and wore his facial hair full and long. Johnson was known as a man who could ride anything with four feet and had been helping Asa Frankmore with his ranch for three years before the man died from old age.

Abe Johnson loved the old man almost as much as he loved the country he settled in. Nevada was wide, wild, open. and free, and that suited him just fine. "I can sit on the back of my wild pony and see mountains a hundred miles away," he'd laugh. He and Asa Frankmore were a real pair. Asa was six foot three and weighed about two hundred fifty pounds, drank whiskey like most men drink water, and worked harder than any five buckaroos. Johnson worked alongside the old gent hour for hour, day for day, and loved every minute of it.

"Well, looky here," Johnson said as Reb rode onto the property. "Reb Sonnett, what brings you out of God's country to mingle with us poor folk? You been riding hard, my friend. Better get that horse took care of right away if you want to be friends with me."

Johnson had a reputation of being an animal's best friend and wouldn't tolerate anyone mistreating any animal. Reb jumped down, breathing hard, and told Abe to follow him, as he led his horse into the barn for water and hay. "We got a much bigger problem than a tired horse, Abe. Another Indian girl has been kidnapped and ravaged."

"My God, no!" Johnson growled. He helped with the horse and the two headed to the main house to talk. "Sounds like Hog Mercer to me."

"Probably, but this time it's a little different. The girl is alive and is being cared for by Ralph Carothers at the East Gate Station."

"I like that ranch. I've hunted the Cold Springs Canyon in the Desatoyas, and that water is the finest in Nevada, I think." He got a fire going and put a pot of coffee on to boil. "Does Crying Wolf know all this?"

"That's why I'm here, Abe. There's a deputy sheriff in from Eureka County, a friend of Carothers, and he thinks it would be best if many of us ranchers gather at East Gate because that's where the girl is. I've been with him for a couple of days and he's pretty damn straight. Even Ma likes him," he chuckled.

"Hell, that says it all, Reb. If the girl's there, why not just give her back?"

"You know that wouldn't work. Crying Wolf will want blood, lots of blood. Corcoran, that's the deputy, thinks the Indians will go for Hog Mercer first. He wants us at East Gate to hold off an area-wide blood-bath in case the Indians go on a killing and burning rampage. You know how they can be when they get their blood up."

"Damn right I know. I've been in more than one Indian fight just comin' west across the prairie. I can't just ride off and leave this place, Reb. I've got animals to feed and tend. This is all I have in the world."

"I know. I know." He gave Abe a sad smile and a pat on the shoulder. "I'm going to get Ma after I leave here. The dogs will keep the sheep safe, but I want her safe, and the safest place for all of us is East Gate. You can't hold off the whole Paiute tribe, Abe. You're all by yourself. Even if they go on a rampage and burn you out, you'll be alive to rebuild." He had a solid argument and Abe Johnson stood near the stove glaring at the boiling coffee and thinking about this ranch he inherited. Six hundred and forty acres of rolling valley floor, a nice herd of cattle, and water. He and Frankmore had hand dug canals to bring water from the Carson River and he grew enough hay to feed the herd all winter if need be.

"Damn that Hog Mercer. His family and Josh Whitney and his family all need to be strung up." He poured coffee for the two of them, pulled a jug from a cabinet and put it on the table. "What about Major Watson? He gonna shut down the stage stop?" When Reb shook his head, he said, "Okay, then, I'll gather my stuff and ride to East Gate."

"Good," Reb said. "I'll ride to get Ma and see you there."

The coffee pot was emptied, the level in that jug

dropped considerably, and the two were on their trails within the hour, but the day was drawing to a close. Both knew they would be making late camps and probably be back on the road well before sunrise. Abe packed a mule for the ride and along with food and extra clothing, had quite an arsenal with him including shotguns, rifles, pistols, and a few sticks of dynamite, just in case.

The drums had been beating their rhythms for two days and Crying Wolf had been building his case before the council of elders. Young painted warriors danced constantly, calling on the gods for victory over the white men who had done such terrible things to little Runs With the Wind. Each time the story was told it got more gruesome.

Every man, woman, and child in the Pyramid Lake tribe of Paiute Indians knew that pretty little girl. She raced dogs and won more often than not. She challenged the young men to races and they often refused not wishing to be whipped by such a skinny little girl. Those that took up the challenge were whipped soundly. Everyone agreed Runs With the Wind got her name honestly.

Crying Wolf was sure that his daughter, who was abducted the year before, had died at the hands of Hog Mercer. He was even more sure that Runs With the Wind had been abused by the filthy white man and his little brother, and finally was given the okay to burn out and kill Hog Mercer and his brother Loren.

Dancing Pines, senior headman since the days of Chief Winnemucca, decreed that other white settlers should be left alone unless they came to the aid of Mercer. "It would be best all around if you could bring those two men here, Crying Wolf. Let our justice prevail. There will be no justice coming from the whites. Paiute justice is final and word of it would spread fear in the hearts of the white man."

"I will form a war party and we will attack. I will do my best to bring Hog Mercer to you, to beg for mercy at your feet. Our warriors can taste the blood of the men who defiled our daughter. Yes, Dancing Pines, I will bring Hog Mercer and fling him at your feet."

The council of elders included Dancing Pines, Shaking Rocks, both of whom agreed to the attack, and others. "Beware, Crying Wolf, of the young men. It will be difficult to hold them back after they taste the sweetness of victory." Shaking Rocks understood a young warrior's desires for continued fighting, continued victories.

The dancing pulsated through the night and as the first light eased the curtain of darkness aside, Crying Wolf rode north along the banks of the Truckee River with fifty men, bound for the Lahontan Valley and the destruction of the Mercer ranch and its owners. He had visions of his elders and ancestors as they fought the white man not that many years ago, felt the power of his ancestors surge through him and sang along with the young men.

Two men flanked Crying Wolf as they rode through rocky country toward the Carson River. Badger, on Crying Wolf's left, was the older one. He was short and squat, his long black hair flowing in the wind. He was a muscular man, short tempered, and filled with hatred of the white man. His family suffered at the hands of the army at the desert lake massacre and he was looking for revenge.

Sings Like the Elk was tall and lithe, hard bodied, fast

on his feet, and able to think most problems through faster than others. He often had Crying Wolf's ear and was hoping this problem with the Mercer boys would end without bringing on a full-scale war with the whites in the area. He wasn't a true peace-maker, planned on killing Hog Mercer himself, but he believed that with some effort the Paiute people could live peacefully with the white people.

"Badger, take two men with you and ride fast toward the Mercer hacienda. Find out how many people are there and bring word back. We don't want to ride into an ambush, and they do know we're coming for them." His snicker told those around him he didn't care how many white men knew he was coming, didn't care how many guns they might have, and was going to kill as many as he could.

"Maybe I'll just ride in and kill them all," Badger said, knowing it would goad Crying Wolf a bit.

"It would be your last ride. Now go."

Badger rode off with two younger men, laughing as a taunt at Crying Wolf. "He needs a good thrashing," Crying wolf muttered. He also knew that he acted that way not too many years ago. "Let's pick up the pace," he chuckled. They dropped down from a high rocky plain to the more verdant Carson River plain where it flowed into the Lahontan Valley. Crying Wolf went out of his way to by-pass Watson's Station.

"Hog Mercer is friends with that Joshua Whitney family, Crying Wolf. Whitney has two sons who often take part in Mercer's cattle rustling and claim jumping." Sings Like an Elk was reminding the leader that this might not be a simple ride in and kill 'em raid, that there might be several guns aimed at them.

"I know. That's why I wanted Badger to find out if Mercer has help. I have been told that Bart Whitney may have been with Loren Mercer when Dancing Pines was attacked. Maybe the other brother too. The elders insist that we are not to burn both ranches, Sings Like the Elk."

"I remember that. Dancing Pines questioned why our beef allotment was shorted, Agent Hatch said nothing, and Whitney attacked the elder. Too many times the white man has insulted us and we've stood silent, Crying Wolf. This feels good, to know we will kill those who disrespect the people and our land."

It was a pleasant ride through the valley, following the twists and turns of the river as it meandered across the wide plain. There were just four or five ranches scattered about, the Mercer place, Whitney's operation, and at the eastern most edge of the plain, where the river ends in a sink, the Frankmore, now Johnson, ranch. There had been others but Mercer had run them off and taken their land. Ranch houses and outbuildings stood empty to the winds and rains. Skeletons of what might have been.

"I want you to take ten men and seal off Mercer's western escape before the night comes on. I'll have another ten on the east, some on the south, and I'll keep the rest with me on the north."

"At sunrise we will attack. No warning, we will ride in from all sides and burn that ranch out, kill those men, and take all the horses and cattle back to Pyramid Lake. At sunrise I'll send one small cloud of smoke. That will be our signal to attack."

"That's a good plan, Crying Wolf. A good plan. If you attack first and pull back, then I'll attack and pull back, then from the west, and finally from the east. I'll put it in operation right now," Sings Like the Elk said. He rode off to assign the warriors, warning them that fires should be small and noise held to nothing.

Groups split off to make their approach to Mercer's place and seal off any escape possibility. Three hours later Badger arrived with some interesting news. "This doesn't change my plans, Badger, but it will make for an interesting sunrise." He spent the next hour or so wondering why the family from the stage stop would partner up with someone like Hog Mercer.

He was standing alongside an ancient cottonwood when Badger approached. "You said the dogs knew you were close. How many dogs, Badger?"

"It sounded like three, maybe more. We left quickly and no one followed. They have many guns but we have many more, Crying Wolf."

"I'm not worried about that," the headman said. "But that family from the stage station shouldn't be here. The white people won't like us killing them. Well," he said, leaning up against the tree, "it was their choice to partner up with the Mercer boys. We attack at sunrise."

When young Reb Sonnett rode off from Watson's Station, the major gave considerable thought to what the man said. "I may have been a bit hasty in chasing that fellow off," he said to his wife, Kendra. Watson's first reaction to just about everything was either no or to run the person suggesting something off. More often than not, on reflection, he would then change his mind. It was a lifelong trait that had caused him many, often serious, problems.

"I'm closing the station until this ugliness passes." He

said. "Find Sandra and get us packed. I detest that Hog Mercer but I can't stand by and let those savages simply ride in and kill him." He only detested the way Mercer treated the Indians. He certainly didn't detest their combined cattle operations.

Here again, the man lied even to himself. He had been working deals and buying and selling stolen cattle and property with the man for more than two years. Working with the Indian Agent, Hatch, they had sweet deals with cattle. Mercer rustled the cattle and he and Watson sold them to Hatch. The government paid full value and Hatch only gave the Indians a small percentage of their allotment, selling the remaining cattle on the open market.

Some were held back and became staples on the Watson Stage Station table. Each of the three, Mercer, Hatch, and Watson made money off the stolen cattle with little or no cost to any of them. Watson was protecting his interests by moving his family to the Mercer ranch to fight alongside his partner, Hog.

"We've not had problems with the Indians, Randall. Why should we now? I don't understand." Kendra Watson was a short, squat, heavy woman in her mid thirties. She was seldom pleased with anything, fawned over Major Watson, tolerated her daughter, and fed bad food to their visitors. "If the Indians want to kill Mr. Mercer, why should we care?"

"That isn't the point, Kendra," Watson snapped. "When the Indians get their blood up, they don't stop killing. They will rampage their way through the Lahontan Valley and we will be their next target. We can't stand alone in this fight. I won't be protecting Mercer as much as I will be protecting our station."

Kendra didn't have a quick mind and Watson's explanation was fuddled to start with. She simply didn't understand his concept of logic but did as he ordered, found their daughter, Sandra, and began packing what few things they would need for a few days at the Mercer ranch.

"What's this all about, Mother? I don't want to be around those filthy men."

"I don't either, honey, but it's what your father wants. He thinks we'll be safer there. What he said was, the Indians think Hog Mercer took a young Indian girl and kept her for a while, then set her loose."

"Well, he's done that before. Indian girls like to be with white men, don't they? I don't want to go."

"You're going whether you want to or not," Major Watson said, walking into the room. "Get your stuff to the barn now. Get it packed on mules. We're leaving in half an hour whether you're ready or not."

Sandra scowled, almost spoke back to her father, thought better of it, and helped her mother. They grabbed what they had put together and carried it to the barn. "Don't get your father riled, Sandra. He gets all riled and takes it out on me. I'll whip you good if I get slapped around because of you." Sandra knew her mother was telling the truth and held her tongue one more time.

Two of the horse boys got the mules packed. "Are they coming with us?" Sandra hoped not. These boys, as they were called, were the sons or hangers-on of those that lived around the stage station hoping to squeeze a little work out of Watson. They cleaned the stalls, maintained the large herd of horses needed, changed teams when stages came through, and did what they could to entice Sandra into a stall, pile of straw, or better yet, their own bed. She was known to tease them unmercifully.

"No. They have to stay here. There will still be stage and road traffic through here."

"But, what about the Indians?"

"Your father thinks the Indians won't hurt the boys. We're leaving them food, after all, and you know they won't do the work they're supposed to do. Let's get our horses out so they can be saddled. I wish we could take the wagon. I hate horses."

"Why aren't we taking the wagon?" Sandra was spoiled and selfish, but was also able to think, probably much more so than her mother. "It would sure be easier than trailing those mules."

"Your father says we need to be able to move quickly and not be forced to stay on roads and trails, which we would if we were in the wagon."

"All right, ladies. That's enough chatter. Let's get mounted and on the road. We can be at the Mercer ranch late this afternoon. No bickering, no arguments, no nonsense, ladies. Let's go."

He led them out of the barn as if they were a military patrol. He was in the lead of course with each of the women trailing a mule. The boys stood in the doorway of the barn watching them go, wondering what was going on. Major Watson hadn't said a word to them or to any of the regular stage line staff.

"Does Pa Hennessy know they are leaving?" One of the boys asked. He didn't wait for an answer, just walked toward the Hennessy shack to tell him. Hennessy was the lead driver on this part of the stage line, from Watson's Station east to Austin. "That miserable coward," Hennessy snarled. "Find my boy, Tommy and bring him here." The stable boy scurried off.

Watson followed the Carson River for about ten miles and turned south toward a line of low hills about five miles away. Kendra had insisted on stopping about every mile or so. She was very overweight and riding a horse was more than uncomfortable. What should have been a four-hour ride turned into a daylong experience. The Mercer ranch was spread out along the base of those hills in some of the driest parts of the wide valley. They kept their herds on land taken from others. They also assumed ownership of water. Hog liked to brag that if a lawman should appear he would never find any mis-branded animals at the ranch.

Hog jumped off the porch of the ramshackle old building and strutted across to where Watson brought his group. He was about thirty years old, scruffy looking with wild long hair, a beard that never took any proper shape, and wore a torn shirt that was not tucked into his trousers. A rifle was carried loosely but Watson noted, ready to be used quickly if needed.

"I heard you were coming, Watson. You give me any trouble, I'll shoot you dead," Hog Mercer said in welcoming. "You're as bad as Josh Whitney, thinkin' them damn savages are gonna attack us. Hell, they ain't ever good enough to fight us. A bunch of horse crap, bringin' your family here."

"The word is that Crying Wolf is already on the trail, Hog. I'm offering my guns just as Josh offered his. Others in the valley are forting up at the East Gate. Maybe I'll take my guns and just ride up there."

"You can stay, Major. Another couple of guns might help, but a few well-placed shots and those Indians will scatter like quail. If they really are coming, they won't be here for at least another couple of days. You know how them damn savages are, drinkin', wantin' them drums goin' all the time."

Watson always called himself Major Watson, but if the truth were known, he was a private in the First Minnesota Volunteers and was mustered out after one of the Pennsylvania fights. A bullet creased his skull and he made them believe that it addled his brain.

Once he got clear of rampaging war, his head seemed to clear right up, and he became a major recovering from serious battle wounds. It got him west, got him a mail contract and Watson's Station is the result. "You got a house full, Hog. We'll settle up in the barn. You made plans for defense? Maybe we should all sit down and think about that. With the Whitney family, your brother, and my guns, we'll be strong if we plan it right."

"It's my place, Major. We do it my way. Get settled and meet us in the big house." Loren interrupted him.

"Scotty just spotted a couple of Injuns down in the cottonwoods, Hog. Dogs smelled 'em first."

"Lookin' to steal cattle. Red bastards. Get your people put together, Major."

"They're here to find out what kind of defense you're putting together, Hog. You'd be wise to kill them before they can report back to Crying Wolf."

"You worry about your family, Major, I'll worry about mine." He and Loren walked off and when they were out of Watson's hearing, Hog told Loren to see if he could chase the two down and kill them.

"Probably gone by now, but I'll give it a try," Loren said, ambling over to where his horse was tied off. He simply rode off across an empty pasture, turned and came back, never attempting to chase down what the dogs sniffed out. The dogs wanted to follow that scent trail but Loren called them off. "Sure don't understand why everybody's afraid of these Indians. Old Major Watson bringing his family here, Slim Nestor riding in to warn Hog, and the Whitney's too."

"I ain't never been afraid of no damn Indian and sure as hell know that Hog ain't."

CHAPTER SIX

"I'm sure glad to see you, Maldonado." Ralph Carothers ushered the Indian agency lawman in. "Jaime, this is Pappy Somerset, an old friend, and one who will stand with us if it comes to that."

The two men shook hands and Pappy gave the Mexican a good look-over, liked what he saw, and everyone sat down in chairs spread out around the large rock fireplace. "Pappy was an army scout many years ago, worked with many of the Plains Indians and was in several battles."

"That was a while back, Ralph. Trackin' and scoutin', well, I'm still fair at, but I'm not much of a fighter at my age," Pappy said.

"Sounds to me like we'll have some good campfire conversations," Maldonado said. "Indian Agency hired me because of some work I did with the Mojave tribes a few years ago."

"Were you able to talk to Crying Wolf?" Carothers asked getting back on track before the two Indian trackers got started on old stories. He thought it was probably a good thing Corcoran wasn't back yet or the stories would go on for days. "Miss Sadie," he hollered toward the kitchen. "Would you get a pot of coffee boiling for us, please. Might sneak that bottle in here, too."

"We talked," Maldonado said, "but I'm afraid there is no more time for talk. He's probably got those young warriors on the path right now. It's unlikely he'll come here to see Runs With the Wind. He has blood and vengeance in his mind and that's all. No, Carothers, it's about to start."

"I sure hope Corcoran gets back. He's had as much dealings with Indians in this country as you," Carothers said. "He has many Paiute and Shoshone friends, and he might be able to keep this ruckus from becoming a full-fledged war."

"For an operating stop, Ralph, you don't have very many people working for you." Pappy Somerset had been thinking about this since he arrived. "You're getting a little age on those bones, pard. Do you do all the work around here?"

"I'm giving up the contract, Pappy. A new station is being organized at the northern part of Cold Spring Canyon, just up the new road from that old Pony Express stop. The new road goes through New Pass instead of over Carroll Summit. I've got one man and his wife left here. They live in a shack out behind the barn. Sadie will be cookin' our supper shortly."

"The old man's pretty much stove up, but he's a good horse man. They'll probably end up at the cold springs station in a month or so." He took a deep breath before continuing. "Unless this war gets started. Two young men work hard with the horses, too. I'm turning this place back to a cattle ranch, which it was supposed to be all along." He sat up suddenly as they all heard boots stomping up the porch stairway and then knocking at the heavy front door.

"Didn't even hear anyone ride in," Pappy said. Carothers walked to the door, his hand near his sidearm, saw Maldonado put his hand over his weapon, and hoped whoever knocked wasn't Indian. He opened the door and found Abe Johnson standing there.

"Abe, my goodness, come in, come in." Carothers turned to the others. "This is Abe Johnson, one of our ranchers from the Lahontan Valley."

"Reb Sonnett will be here shortly with his mother," Johnson said. "He also said another man, a deputy sheriff from Eureka would be here, too."

Johnson hadn't quite finished speaking when Terrence Corcoran stepped through the door. "Now we got enough for a party," he said. He walked to the fire, pulled out of his coat, and warmed his hands. "Pappy Somerset, is that you? Well, damn me, I'm glad to see your rotten hide. What brings you here?"

Pappy threw his arms around his old friend and squeezed him tight. "Ralph's an old friend and I just stopped to say hello. He told me all about what's going on so I stayed to see if I can help. I'm sure glad to see you, Terrence Corcoran. Life in the Monitor Valley is dull without you around," he laughed.

Miss Sadie hollered from the kitchen that supper was on the table and the men headed that way. "Glad I made a big pot of stew, Ralph. My goodness, we have quite a crowd for supper. Settle in, boys, I've got dried apple pie for later."

"Looks like one of my calves was sacrificed for this stew." A Dutch oven sat on the table with enough food for the Seventh Cavalry if they should happen by. "She's a fine cook but doesn't much like to carry on a conversation," he chuckled. She gave the old man a pat on the shoulder and a big smile.

"I remember you liking to carry on with pretty girls, Mr. Carothers," Pappy Somerset snickered. "That might have something to do with her lack of conversation." Carothers just harrumphed some and ladled out a bowl full of stew.

Bowls were filled and chairs occupied in short order. A platter of biscuits was emptied and talk of Indian war filled the air. "Tell me more about this Crying Wolf, Jaime," Corcoran said. "Is he the kind of man that someone could talk with?"

"He is. So is one of the elders, Dancing Pines. I'm afraid Crying Wolf isn't going to be the problem once this thing starts. Many of the young warriors have heard stories of fights with the white man's armies, posses, and raiders, and they have never had the experience. They smell blood, Corcoran. God help us when they get their first taste of it."

More pounding at the door brought the conversation to a stop and Carothers answered it with men standing behind him, weapons at the ready. "This is a fine welcome," Sarah Sonnett said, seeing five men with guns standing in the middle of the living room. "Glad I'm a peaceful old widow woman." She laughed and walked up to

Ralph and gave him a hug. "Hello, Corcoran. This your army?"

He chuckled, looked around the room, and stepped forward, bowed slightly and took her hand. "I believe it's the finest fighting outfit in central Nevada, Mrs. Sonnett."

"We were just eating, Mrs. Sonnett. Will you and Reb join us?" Ralph Carothers led the party back to the kitchen. The table was large enough to accommodate the group. "We were talking about Crying Wolf. You've had dealings with the man."

"I have," she said. "He's an intelligent, willful man, but has empathy for his people, understands far better than most how the throngs of immigrants have changed the lives of his people. He's angry, as he has every right to be, but also has a desire to work with the whites if it is in the best interest of his people."

She took a pause, a reflective moment before continuing. "We must remember that a little girl, related to him, was abducted and murdered recently and the white community has done nothing about that. Now, another young girl has been viciously attacked and left to die in the desert. The man must be in a rage, and he has the charisma and the authority to lead warriors. I doubt we could talk him out of taking out his hatred on Hog Mercer."

"That's well said," Corcoran said. "I just hope he can control those riding with him. If what Jaime Maldonado just told us is right, Hog Mercer won't have a ranch this time tomorrow and we might be in the line of fire. The little girl in the back bedroom will bring him here."

"I've had more than one conversation with the man," Sarah Sonnett said. "Family is at the root of the man. He looks at the whole of the Paiute tribe as family and what happened to little Runs With the Wind will keep him in a rage for a long time. Maybe, I don't know, but maybe knowing she's alive and doing well will ease the pressure some."

Sarah had been talking directly to Corcoran, not looking around the room at all, and he could see a strong woman, still more than attractive, and one fully capable of making decisions. "If that was my daughter back there, or even a shirt-tail relative, I'd be in a rage," he said. "I'm going to ride to the Mercer place tomorrow and find that gentleman, and bring this to an end."

It was very quiet at that table as his words sunk in. "A white man is going to ride to an Indian raid on a white ranch to talk to the head Indian?" Death warrants handed down by judges aren't any more guaranteed than this one. Corcoran would not let something as horrible as what happened to the little girl simply go by the wayside. The war must end and girl must be protected.

"Someone should ride with you, Terrence," Pappy Somerset said. "Someone like me, for instance."

"I was going to bring Runs With the Wind," he said.

"Then it will be I riding with you, Mr. Corcoran," Sarah said.

"And I," Pappy said. "No one else, though or Crying Wolf will get the wrong idea. We must ride in peace and carry with us the one thing he's fighting for."

There were arguments back and forth, for and against, for the next couple of hours but Corcoran's idea was the only one he would accept. "If what Sarah said is true, that Crying Wolf's whole purpose is to protect family, that is, tribe, then he will welcome us bringing him his little girl."

Abe Johnson and Reb Sonnett argued long that they should be included. Sonnett did not want his mother riding in the party and Johnson offered the strength of giants. Both men were told no.

With Sarah and Pappy backing Corcoran with equally strong arguments, the plan developed. "We'll leave out of here just at daybreak and it will take at least the entire day to make the ride. It's a long hard ride and we'll be riding into great danger at its end."

"Runs With the Wind needs to know our plan, needs to understand why we're doing this," Sarah said.

"I've talked with her, Sarah," Jaime Maldonado said. "She's a pretty sharp little girl. She's been terribly abused but she's strong and willing to come with us. She has one big time crush on a certain deputy sheriff that saved her life."

The laughter eased the tense situation and plans were made for the ride. "We'll need food for the ride to and from Mercer's place," Corcoran said. "I would like to make it there in one day, but we should plan for the worst."

"It's about fifty miles, Corcoran," Carothers said. "It would easier if you planned on two days."

"Easy on us? Who cares," Corcoran said. "Our job is to stop a war. We'll leave at four, Pappy. All three of us have good strong horses and we'll ride light."

Carothers and Pappy headed for the barn well before first light to make up the pack for the mule they would need while Reb Sonnett and Abe Johnson continued to put pressure on Sarah and Corcoran to let them come. "You'll need us, Ma," Reb pleaded. "You can't just ride out with those two men. You'll need our protection."

"I know how you feel, son, but Terrence is right. We must give the impression of peace. If we show up with an armed guard Crying Wolf will respond in kind. Showing up with a woman, a child, and one other man will give Corcoran the advantage of coming in peace. I'm sure you can understand that."

"I'm afraid I do, Ma. I just don't want to," he chuckled. "You're all I've got and I'm not willing to let you ride off as an avenging angel or something."

"We've had Crying Wolf at our supper table, Reb. You know the man. He has deep feelings for his people and their ways. We are bringing him an offering not a threat. Whether or not he can control the young hot-heads is another story."

"That's the one I'm afraid of."

Sarah Sonnett was a trail wise ranch woman, spent hours in the saddle moving cattle and sheep, fought off wolves and marauding cougars, fought off Indian attacks, and was more than capable of making this effort on behalf of all the ranchers in that part of central Nevada. "You and Abe need to stay here with Ralph and Jaime. What Terrence and I are doing might just save our ranches."

Sonnet picked up on his mother calling Corcoran by his first name immediately and got a little grin on his face. "So, it's Terrence is it?" She took a swat at him but couldn't hide her own grin. "Are you going to retire that tin star he wears?" She didn't answer her son but carried that smile for a few more moments.

"All right, let's mount up and get this show on the road," Corcoran said. He had Runs With the Wind wrapped in a blanket and when he climbed into the saddle, she had her arms wrapped tightly around his neck.

"Looks like you've got some competition there, Ma," Reb Sonnett laughed. She growled a bit, but there was that smile on her face as they rode west from East Gate.

"We're going to have to spend the night on the trail aren't we, Terrence?" She asked as they rode side by side.

"That mule will slow us down considerably, Sarah. Mules are strong and he could probably out work any one of these horses, but they aren't fast on the trail. We'll get as close to Mercer's ranch as we can before nightfall. I sure don't want to ride into a war party after the sun goes down." They laughed at the thought, but it was tinged with thoughts of ugly death.

"Have you ever been married?" Sarah knew she was getting mighty personal but the man intrigued her.

"Almost. Once. Thought about it a time or two. Thought about ranching some. Don't think I'm gonna, though." The conversation ended but the two of them had their own thoughts rambling around for several more miles. She wondered what kind of man Terrence Corcoran really was and he contemplated actually settling down in one place with one woman for the rest of his life.

"It's coming light," Badger said, nudging Crying Wolf. "It's a good day to fight."

"Yes, it is. That man will never abuse another young girl, ever. Make the men ready and get ready to send up the smoke to alert the others. Have you heard from any of the other scouts?"

"No, and that means everything is quiet at the ranch."

The plan was a simple one. Crying Wolf would attack from the north first drawing all the defenders toward him. Then Sings Like an Elk would attack from the south hopefully causing chaos in the defenders. At that point, men on the east side would attack, and just a few minutes after that, the attack from the west would start.

"All we'll see is blood and smoke in an hour, Badger." Crying Wolf carried a wet blanket to the fire, put some fresh pine boughs on the fire and covered it with the blanket for a few long seconds. When he pulled the blanket back a thick cloud of smoke rose on the morning air carrying the signal to attack.

Crying Wolf led his screaming braves through the heavy brush and trees and into the main yard of the Mercer ranch. They rode their ponies hard, firing into the ramshackle ranch house at will. They circled the building twice before a second group came in with their torches, flinging them through broken windows, onto the porch, and arcing high onto the roof.

Crying Wolf signaled the men to fall back to the brush and trees and take up positions to fire on the house and barns. The youngest braves were given the jobs of keeping the horses back and out of danger from the return gunfire.

Watson, Kendra, and Sandra were sleeping in the main barn and came out of their blankets fast when the first horrible screams of the Paiute warriors echoed through the old wood. "Indians," Watson hollered, reaching for his rifle. The gunfire from the invaders was random and bullets were flying in every direction.

"Stay on the ground and in those stalls," Watson yelled, trying to get free from his blanket. He moved toward the big open doorway and saw twenty or more braves on horseback racing around the ranch, firing into the house and the outbuildings. Visions of what happened in Pennsylvania flashed through his mind, and he once again froze like the coward he was. This was the true meaning of fear.

He simply stood in the open doorway, rifle at his side. He couldn't move and a bullet tore through his left arm, turning him completely around with its force. He dropped the rifle, fell to the ground, shaking, almost crying out in panic.

Kendra screamed in horror when he fell to the ground. Sandra was buried in her blankets, sobbing in fright. "Randall," Kendra screamed over and over, too frightened to move. She saw him move, try to crawl back from the door and saw Indians advancing on him.

He saw rebels coming toward him with bayonets fixed to their long rifles. He tried to crawl back into the barn when three more bullets ripped his life away.

Kendra was screaming, cowering in her blanket, holding on to a supporting post, and saw Watson thrash some, then lay still. Sandra cried out when Watson lay crumpled on the ground and wanted to rush to his side but was too frightened to even move. Two warriors rode into the barn, saw the women and one raised his war ax.

"No," commanded a voice from behind him. "Take them to the brush and wait there. Do not harm those women." Crying Wolf rode out of the barn and continued firing his rifle into the big house.

When the warriors took their positions in the brush, they began their systematic firing at the ranch house, getting some sporadic return fire. "Keep those women safe. No harm is to come to them," Crying Wolf said again. "Let those men in the house feel the flames we've offered, and come to these windows to shoot at us. Soon, Sings Like an Elk will attack from the other side." There was general laughter along the line of fire as the braves put scores of bullets through old and dry wooden walls.

"What the hell?" Hog Mercer came up from a drunken sleep, awakened by horrible screaming from outside his bedroom window. "Indians!" He yelled, jumping from his bed. Several bullets crashed through the glass as he struggled into his boots. He found his rifle and rushed to the window in time to see painted, howling, Indian warriors riding through the barnyard, shooting into the house. Some brandished flaming torches, others carried war clubs and axes. Many were armed with rifles, some with bows and arrows.

"No," he stammered, pulling his rifle and taking a wild shot at a rider passing quickly in front of the window. Many of the attacking warriors carried bows and arrows and were deadly with them. "Loren," he howled for his brother. Last night he laughed when Slim Nestor told him to fort up because the Indians were coming. Nestor left before the Indian sighting.

Hog Mercer tried to sulk behind the wall, away from the window but wasn't fast enough. An arrow stung its way into his shoulder, buried deep in flesh and bone, and he fell to the floor in pain. Blood was streaming from the wound when Loren Mercer came running in. He fell to help his brother. "Kill them red bastards," Hog yelled. "Kill them." Loren ran to the window, his revolver in hand.

Loren Mercer watched as the Indians pulled back and into the brush that surrounded the wide yard area. He picked Hog's rifle up, took a couple of shots and didn't hit anything. Return fire was immediate and he dove to the floor. "Must be the whole damn Paiute tribe, Hog. You said they wouldn't be here until tomorrow."

"Get that arrow out before I bleed to death you idiot." Josh Whitney and his sons, Bart and Sam came running in. "Kill them red savages," Hog yelled again. He was writhing in pain when Loren tried to pull the arrow out of solid bone.

"Get out of the way," Josh Whitney said, shoving the younger Mercer aside. "Hang on, Hog," he said. He put a foot against Mercer's chest, grabbed the arrow and gave a mighty yank on the shaft, ripping it out of bone and muscle. Hog Mercer fainted from the extreme pain. "Now, let's kill us some Indians," Whitney said.

There were two windows in the room and two men with rifles at each one. "I can't see them," Sam Whitney cried out. "They's firin' at us but I cain't see 'em."

"Just shoot where them puffs of smoke are. Damn you are stupid sometimes," Joshua said.

Several of the rooms in the ranch house were on fire from thrown torches, the roof was burning as well, and as the four men continued to shoot toward the line of brush to their north, horses streamed out of the woods to the south and Sings Like an Elk led some twenty warriors in their attack on that side of the house.

"My God, how did they get around there?" Loren ran across to the other side of the house and saw mounted Indians firing into the open windows, throwing burning torches into and on top of the house. "We got to get out of here," he screamed, bolting to the front door.

"Don't leave me," Hog Mercer cried out. "You little

bastard, don't leave me." Josh Whitney jerked the crying man to his feet, slapped him hard across his tear-stained face, and pushed him toward the door.

"Just a damned coward," he snarled, giving him a second shove. Hog tripped on something, didn't fall, and tried to run toward the door. Loren was knelt to the side of the door, his rifle barking loud, shot after shot.

"They gotta be five hunnert of them savages, Hog. Pull your damn gun and shoot," he said.

They had other weapons spread around the house but were unable to get to them or the extra ammunition. One by one, the defenders ran out of ammunition. Josh Whitney in a last attempt to kill an Indian raced toward one on a horse. The warrior swung his war ax and cleaved Whitney's head in two. Sam ran from the house and took two arrows through his chest, falling dead at his father's side.

Within three or four minutes the forces from the east and west converged on the ranch house, rifles and bows at the ready, but Crying Wolf had signaled no more shooting. He mounted his pony and rode across the broad barnyard to where three white men were being held by snarling warriors. They were screaming for the kill but Crying Wolf kept indicating no, he wanted them alive, at least for the time being.

Loren Mercer was standing with Hog and Bart Whitney, who was suffering from a gunshot to the leg. He crumpled half way to the ground, holding tightly to Loren. Crying Wolf rode his pony slowly around the three, calling out their crimes in Paiute. He put it in a chant, and many of his warriors joined in.

Crying Wolf pulled his horse to a stop and slipped off

to stand in front of the three white men. He carried a stone headed war club and swung a mighty arc, crushing Bart Whitney's head. Loren gasped as blood and brains were splashed onto the dirt and dust of the barnyard.

"You two will not be so lucky," Crying Wolf cried out. "You will understand our pain, miserable devils that you are. You have defiled our children, our young girls, you have stolen our cattle, killed our people, and you will not die honorably." He was howling the words to the winds of the desert and his warriors began to dance as a drum started pounding out a driving rhythm.

The Indians pummeled the men as they rode by, Crying Wolf making sure none of the blows were lethal. Each man had his opportunity, each said vile things to the crying men. After more than an hour of physical abuse the two were hauled away.

Sings Like an Elk had the Mercer brothers tied to cottonwood trees, their arms stretched wide, their legs spread painfully as other warriors went from room to room of the ranch house building fires. The structure was old and weathered and burned furiously in a strong wind that had built as the day wore on.

Badger brought a well fed steer to their little camp and it was slaughtered, the meat spread among the men. Fires were lit and the men stopped dancing long enough to eat, then back to dancing and chanting. "We have stopped the men who have been abusing our girls and women," Badger said. "Now, we march on the others. Watson's Station isn't far from here." He was laughing, gnawing on a rib bone, and dancing to the drums.

"And, the Frankmore ranch is closer," a young warrior said. "These white ranchers must die," he howled.

"No!" Crying Wolf stood near the main fire where the drums were. He looked to the men at the drums and they ceased their play. In the quiet the men gathered around their headman thinking he would give the order to continue the attacks. "It will take at least two days for these two men to die for what they have done. The other ranchers are to be spared. Knowing what we have done to these two will keep others from wanting to follow their treacherous ways.

"No!" He was more than emphatic and said, "the other whites will live."

Grumbling went on for some time as the drums began their ritualistic beat, men danced war dances, blood running hot, and Crying Wolf knew he would have a hard time keeping his word that no more whites were to be killed. He called Sings Like an Elk and Badger to his fire.

"I gave my word to the elders that we would only burn the Mercer ranch. My word," he said again. He looked hard at Badger, knowing the man's hatred of the whites. "I will not return to Pyramid Lake and tell Dancing Pines, Shaking Rocks, and the others that I failed."

"The young men did not give their word," Badger muttered.

Crying Wolf looked at his long time friend with pleading eyes but knew in his heart that he had lost the argument. Sings Like the Elk never said a word.

CHAPTER SEVEN

Smoke from the burning Mercer ranch house could be seen for miles in the flat Lahontan Valley and Corcoran spotted the first wisps from far off. "We're too late to save the Mercer's," he grumbled, "but we may still be able to talk to Crying Wolf."

It was mid-afternoon of their second day on the trail and the three riders could feel the tension of what might lie in front of them. Every bush might conceal danger or death, every rock outcrop might hide twenty ferocious savages, and every dust devil might indicate a horde riding toward them. And that's when Corcoran pointed out the smoke in the distance.

They rode quietly, stunned at the intensity of the fire still many miles in front of them. "Every building on that ranch must be aflame," Pappy Somerset said. "Who would have been with those men, Sarah?"

"I'm sure the Whitney family would be there, but I can't imagine anyone else willing to stand with vermin like them. Do you have a plan, Corcoran? We'll be mighty close in an hour."

"Jaime said Crying Wolf would have at least fifty men with him, so finding his camp will be the easy part. Getting in to talk with him will be difficult. I know less than five words of Paiute, but this little angel in my arms is going to be our ticket in. She's bruised, her head must still hurt like the dickens, but she has Crying Wolf's heart and our entrée."

"Sure hope he's right," Pappy murmured, catching Sarah's eye. He had so many bad encounters with Indians in his background, had ridden with so many young army officers who were so sure of themselves that entire companies of men died, but he also had ridden with Corcoran before. No one but the bad guys died, he remembered.

Was he right agreeing to leave Jaime Maldonado behind. After all, Jaime spoke the language, knew Crying Wolf personally, and yes, there was the fact he represented the Indian bureau. "Well," he murmured to himself, "if I'm going to die, I'll be with a lovely lady and my good friend, Corcoran."

They moved through the open plain, broken by some run-off ditches, a few stands of brush, and rolling hills of sandy dirt. "We're getting close, so keep your eyes open and your hands away from your weapons," Corcoran said. What was left of the Mercer ranch was close now, still blazing, filling the air with filthy smoke.

They were about half a mile out when four painted warriors rode up from an arroyo with rifles cocked and pointed. The four rode around the little party, shaking their rifles, screaming insults, but letting them continue forward. "I have the feeling we're expected," Corcoran smiled. "I wonder how long someone has been following us?" He held little Runs With the Wind, but she was squirming around enough for the blanket to fall halfway from her shoulders.

The insults flailing the spring time air were spoken in her language and she tried to get free from the blankets. Not free from this huge man who saved he life, but out of the blankets to see who was saying these horrible things. Her pretty little face emerged from the blankets, her eyes wide open.

The warriors stopped howling, stopped the horses, and one rode up close and said something, almost softly. She answered with dancing eyes and a big smile. The Indian, painted for war looked at Corcoran, nodded, and motioned for the party to follow.

"Round one goes to our little friend here," he said to Sarah who was riding alongside. "Let's hope our luck holds." Runs With the Wind was sitting up much straighter as they rode, but never let go of Corcoran. Even when she was talking with the fierce warrior she held tight to this big white man. She laid her head on his chest and watched the warriors lead them toward their camp.

Sarah had seen that from the time they left the ranch. "That girl can't see color, doesn't give a damn where you're from Corcoran. God, wouldn't it be something if we could all be like that?" She alternated between scowls and smiles, looking at Terrence, many years her junior, and wondering just what kind of man he really was. That he was a man, there was no doubt, but they came in so many guises. He was soft and warm with that little girl, an open faced flirt with her, and, she saw, he had the eye of a killer when that was called for.

It was the badge that separated him from the likes of the Mercer boys, she thought. "You ever thought of giving up that badge of yours, Terrence?"

He looked over at her with just the hint of a smile. "Once," is all he said, and she could see he wasn't going to expand on that one word.

"Must have been one hell of woman," she muttered, letting her eyes roam over the lawman. For the next few minutes she tried her best to picture Corcoran spending his days with cattle, sheep, and irrigation ditches and almost laughed right out loud at the picture. "Ain't gonna happen," she whispered.

"Do you have any idea what those two said to each other, Pappy?" Corcoran knew the older man spoke some Indian talk.

"No. Paiute ain't the same as Sioux. I can get along some in sign but not in words. We should have brought Jaime."

"His position with the Indian Agency would not have been to our advantage, Pappy. We talked about that. He would be good for talking, but Crying Wolf would see him as someone from the Indian Agency. Just another white man's tool. Hopefully we're not looked on that way, too. She knew that warrior and whatever she said, was to our favor."

The three, along with the little girl rode into a large camp, led by two warriors in front and two more behind. The rowdy camp slowly got very quiet as they made their way to Crying Wolf's fire. There were two white men tied to trees, bloody, and badly injured. Corcoran also saw two white women, not tied, but cowering under the supervision of several warriors.

"Those women are Major Watson's wife and daughter," Sarah whispered to Corcoran. "I can't imagine why they would be here."

One warrior jumped from his horse while the other three kept close watch on Corcoran and company. He strode to the fire as Crying Wolf got to his feet. He spoke rapidly with Crying Wolf, using his hands as emphasis often. Crying Wolf looked to Corcoran, then to Sarah, and finally to Runs With the Wind. The headman nodded a couple of times as the warrior continued speaking.

Grim faced warriors, weapons held ready for instant use surrounded the three, and many pointed to the little girl who was holding tightly to Corcoran, but smiling back at the men. "There's a lot of love for this little girl," Sarah said. "These men were here to seek justice from those that harmed her. Seeing her alive and well might contain their anger and frustration."

"Damn me, but I hope you're right," Corcoran chuckled. "Looks like Crying Wolf is headed our way."

Crying Wolf had been standing with his long lance in hand, set it aside, and motioned to Sings Like an Elk to do the same. The two men, almost in a swagger, made their way through the throng of painted warriors to Corcoran's horse. He ignored Corcoran and spoke directly to the little girl.

"We have the men who hurt you," he said in Paiute. "You have been treated well by these people?" She nodded. His grim face slowly eased when she smiled at him and said this man holding her saved her life. Crying Wolf motioned for Corcoran and the others to dismount and join him at his fire.

"Round two," Sarah whispered, stepping off her horse.

Runs With the Wind held tightly to Corcoran as he led the little group following Crying Wolf through the massed warriors, all primed for more killing, more blood. "Good plan, Terrence," she said to his returned chuckle.

Crying Wolf led them to where the Mercer brothers were tied to the trees. He pointed to them and asked Runs With the Wind if she knew them. She nodded and said, in Paiute, "Yes. Those men are the ones who kidnapped me," and she started crying hard, hiding her face in the blanket wrapped around her, and clinging desperately to Corcoran.

Corcoran didn't have to understand the language to know what was asked and what the answer had been. Crying Wolf stood straight and looked deep into the eyes of the man holding the little girl. "I'm going to say this twice, white man. First in your tongue, then in mine. Listen closely, white man, for I believe you and I are on the same trail." He turned and opened his arms wide and gestured for silence. He began in English, one phrase, then repeated in Paiute until he was finished.

"Then let it be known that we, warriors from the Paiute Nation, have brought the right men to face our justice. We have burned their ranch to the ground, killed those that stood with them, and will bring these miserable examples of white men to our lake home to face the wrath of our women."

He wasn't necessarily speaking to the three whites standing before him, Corcoran realized immediately. Crying Wolf was an astute leader and was telling his braves, these men who looked to him as their leader, that they had accomplished what they set out to do. He would not ride through the Lahontan Valley and the basin and range area of Nevada and wreak havoc among the white settlers.

"Round three," Corcoran whispered to Sarah who gave him the slightest smile. Some men are fighters just because of the fight, others fought when ordered to do so without feelings or thought. Corcoran saw a third type of fighting warrior in Crying Wolf; the kind who felt a passion for a cause, whether it be the people he defended, the idea that needed his help, or for a type of justice. He doubted though that this Paiute headman could hold the young men seeking more than justice. They had their first taste of hot blood.

The assembled warriors were slow to grasp the meaning of Crying Wolf's words and many were anticipating burning the ranches of the whites in the area, killing as many white men as they could find, seeking their brand of justice. Vengeance was still thirsty and felt unfulfilled.

Pappy saw it first and Corcoran saw him visibly tighten up as he looked out at the almost fifty faces looking back. Crying Wolf would have a hard time keeping this army under control. It was about to turn from organized battle group to mob and all it would take would be someone with enough charisma to light the fire. Pappy Somerset stepped just a bit closer to Sarah, forcing her to get closer to Corcoran. "Stay very close," he whispered, just loud enough for the three of them to hear.

The general mumbling among the braves got louder, some crying out their frustration, some asking why this should be the end of their hunt for vengeance, some seeming gratified that it was over and they and Runs With the Wind were safe. Crying Wolf paced back and forth, his lance back in hand, glaring at those complaining, daring them to challenge his authority.

Crying Wolf had been at the desert lake massacre after the fact, to clean up what the army had done. The army still existed in Nevada, no longer at Fort Churchill, but still up north at Fort McDermott, and they could be here in three days or less. He had to keep these pent up young men under control. Again, Crying Wolf stopped, raised his arms wide, and quieted the crowd.

"We have done what we came to do," he said in Paiute. "Runs With the Wind is safe, the men who abused her so viciously are ours, and every white person within four suns of where we stand will cower at what we've done. We are not the savages the whites believe we are. We, as the whites like to say about themselves, only seek justice for crimes committed against us."

"We will feast and dance in victory tonight and make the glorious trek home tomorrow, knowing our hearts are pure, and our pride is proper. The whites will tremble remembering today and our women will be safe. Our homes will be warm. We will drive the cattle of these men to our pastures and remember how they cowered before us."

"Sure wish to hell I knew what he was saying," Corcoran said. "He's sure got their attention." Many of the warriors were ready to go home. Some nursed wounds that needed attention, but there were those few who smelled blood. They had their first taste and wanted more.

Crying Wolf turned to Corcoran. "You are to be given safe passage, Terrence Corcoran. On behalf of my people, thank you for saving this child. Go now, in peace. You will not be harmed." He reached out for Runs With the Wind, still clinging to her savior. She loved and trusted the fierce looking Paiute headman and slowly released her hold on Corcoran. She was crying and smiling as Crying Wolf held her up for the warriors to see.

The cheering erupted and Crying Wolf nodded to Corcoran as if to say, go now, white man, while you can. "I want to, Crying Wolf," Corcoran said, and pointed across the open space to the two white women. "What about them? I understand they are from Watson's Station. The stage stop."

"Their man was fighting with the Mercer brothers, Terrence Corcoran. We don't want them," he said with a slight nod. "Unlike your army, Paiutes do not kill women and children." He made a few gestures and the women were bundled aboard a couple of broken down horses captured from the Mercer corrals. "Take them and leave."

Corcoran nudged Sarah, Pappy was already half way in the saddle, and within seconds two warriors led them through the still cheering throng and out into the gathering twilight. Corcoran was leading the horse that Kendra Watson rode while Pappy Somerset led the horse carrying Sandra. Both women were sobbing, unsure of their balance, riding without benefit of saddle or bridle.

When they were some three miles out their escort turned back. One gave the traditional upraised open hand, the other simply scowled. Corcoran and Pappy nodded and saluted back, not slowing down. Sarah turned in the saddle and watched as the two loped back toward the Paiute camp.

"Can he hold them?" Pappy asked and already knew the answer. "There will be at least ten of them in paint and screaming for blood before the night is over, Terrence."

Corcoran just nodded as he put his horse in a strong trot working to get as many miles as possible from Crying Wolf's camp before it was too dark to ride. "We'll try to make the river, Pappy. We'll be safe there. Even the hotheads aren't angry at us."

"So far," the old scout laughed. "You better slow it down, old man. These women sure as hell ain't riders and that big one's about to take a tumble."

"We came on the trail because of the slow mule and we're going home because of women who can't ride horses. What did you call this, Sarah? My army?" Corcoran had to laugh and it was contagious with Pappy and Mrs. Sonnett. Corcoran knew the tension of the situation was easing and hoped that Crying Wolf could hold his wild braves for several more hours.

They slowed back to a walk and Sarah Sonnett rode up next to Sandra. "What were you doing at that ranch, Sarah? I thought your father detested Hog Mercer." The girl was sobbing uncontrollably, holding the horse's mane with both hands. Her face was streaked with ash, her dress ripped, and her arms and legs bruised from being manhandled into the woods.

She either couldn't or wouldn't answer, but Sarah wanted an answer. "My son, Reb, went to see your father and was all but run off, Sandra. Has your father been working with Hog Mercer all this time? Is he a cattle rustler, too? Did he help kidnap that little girl?"

Sarah Sonnett was far more than angry and wanted to slap the girl into answering. "You cannot deny that you, your mother, and your father were at the Mercer ranch to help defend Hog. Crying Wolf is showing a side of an Indian I've never seen before, letting you and your mother ride off with us. If your father has been riding with Hog Mercer, and you were at the ranch defending Hog, I hope Jaime Maldonado puts you under arrest for crimes against the Paiute nation."

The sobs turned to wails that filled the air and could probably be heard for a mile or more. Pappy Somerset reached out and slapped the girl hard, ending the outcry. "Any more of that nonsense, girl, and I'll fill your mouth with a filthy kerchief and tie it tight." Screaming like that could bring the Indians back at a hard gallop. They needed distance and quiet before any uprising that might take place. Pappy nudged his horse and jerked on the lead line forcing Sandra's horse into a slow trot. Her mind quickly turned to holding on, not crying out in fear.

"Do you suppose the Indians rode through Watson's Station before attacking the Mercer ranch?" Sarah asked as she rode up next to Corcoran.

"Not likely," he said. "That man carried a load of arrogance that was hefty and well established. I don't think he was tied in with the Mercers, though. Unlike what you saw in that little girl, he saw color and hated anything that wasn't white. I don't think he was a criminal in that sense of the word but he had his values more than misplaced in my opinion. Hell, maybe Hog Mercer called to him for help." Corcoran wasn't aware of the bond between Mercer, Watson, and the Indian Agent, Hatch.

"I guess we'll never know that," she said. "Let's find that camp soon, Terrence. What a day." She had a smile though and color in her cheeks. Corcoran saw a strong woman who would be more than able to defend herself, her ranch, and her son.

What would my life be like if I had a woman like that by my side? I'm sure the badge would disappear first. His thoughts brought a chuckle and Sarah looked over at him, almost questioned the chuckle and decided against it. He would be somebody's catch some day, she thought, but not hers.

"If we don't find a campsite soon these women are gonna just fall off the damn horses, Terrence," Pappy snarled, getting everyone's mind back on the business at hand.

CHAPTER EIGHT

Pappy shot a couple of sage grouse, Sarah had a fire started, and the two Watson women sat under a cottonwood tree, whimpering. There were open welts on their wrists from rope burns, numerous cuts and bruises, and neither one seemed capable of helping in any way. Pappy was scornful while Sarah had tried but got nothing back from either woman.

"When I was a pup," Pappy said, "women on the frontier were tougher'n most of the men. Can't tolerate a whimperin' woman. Get 'em up and get 'em workin' and they won't have time for any damn whimperin'."

"Getting a bit crotchety in your old age there, Pappy," Corcoran chuckled. He was bringing in more wood, as a young boy, about fourteen years old, riding a large plow horse rode up. "Hello the camp," he yelled in a voice that hadn't quite turned over to a man's.

"Come on in, boy. Most of us are friendly," Pappy Somerset laughed. "That's quite a horse you're ridin'." He thought pulling a plow would more suit that animal. The boy was riding bareback and his legs were well spread to the sides.

"Tommy," Kendra Watson yelled out. "Tommy Hennessy. What are you doing here?"

"You know this boy?" Pappy Somerset helped the youngster stand up straight after he made the jump down from the tall plow horse. 'That your name, son?"

"Yes. My father's a stage driver and sent me to find Mr. Carothers at East Gate. Something's wrong at Watson's Station."

"I bet there is," Pappy growled. He walked the boy to the fire, indicated everyone should sit down, including the two Watson women. "Time for some answers, I think," the old scout said. Corcoran loved the little smile that went with it. "We'll have coffee ready in a minute son, so start talking."

"When my pa brought the Carson stage in from Dayton, there were no fresh horses, none of the horse boys were around the station, and he couldn't find anyone inside either."

"Had the Indians been there?" Corcoran was afraid if they had hit the station before attacking Hog Mercer's ranch, then the other ranchers would be next for sure.

"Pa called me to the station, we live several hundred yards away, and told me to ride like the fires of Hades was following me to East Gate. I didn't see no arrows or nothing. Nothing was on fire and there weren't no bodies in the dirt bleedin'." The boy's eyes were wide, maybe excitement, probably not fear, Sarah Sonnett noticed.

"So them vile boys deserted our station," Kendra Watson snarled.

"Yeah," Sarah Sonnett snarled back. "Just like you and

your husband did." She noticed that neither one of the Watson women had asked if anyone was hurt. Sarah was a ranch widow who saw to it that things got done. These two were takers not givers. "You got more to say, Tommy?"

Tommy Hennessy was fourteen, short and heavy, not with fat, and probably as strong as a man. While his father drove the stage routes across Nevada, connecting many of the little farming and mining communities not tied into the big railroads to the north, he stayed home running the farm and taking care of his mother and little brother.

"Them boys that Major Watson hired to take care of the horses run off to Dayton or Virginia City, I guess." He looked around at the two battered women. "Probably as soon as the Major run off." Kendra Watson wanted to say something but the look from Sarah Sonnett changed her mind. "Ma and me had heard there might be Indians comin' but they come by all the time anyway. Ain't no reason to run off like that."

"We didn't run off, Tommy. The Major went to help a friend," Kendra snapped.

"So the Watson family and the Mercer boys were friends, eh?" Pappy Somerset said. "I wonder what happens to Watson's Station now?"

"There's a contract with the stage line and the U.S. Mail that might be available if you're looking to settle down, Pappy," Corcoran laughed.

"I'd as soon jump into those fires of Hades the boy was runnin' from, Terrence." Pappy turned to the boy. "We'll be riding into East Gate tomorrow, Tommy. You're welcome to ride with us, that is if we still have our scalps."

. . .

Ralph Carothers was pacing around the corrals, kicking at the dirt once in a while, cussing a blue streak often, and finally strode into the barn. "I tell you, Reb, they rode off to get themselves kilt, sure as I'm standing here."

"Take it easy, Ralph. They should be back sometime late today is what I'm thinkin'. What's got you buggered is the fact the Carson stage is late. That stage was due this morning. Not knowin' something is worse than knowin' I think. Let's go in the house and see what Jaime thinks."

"Yeah, let's do that," Carothers said. "Get Miss Sadie to fix us some coffee."

"You as sweet on her as she is on you?" Reb had a smile on his face remembering how his mother once thought the old man might come calling on her.

"I ain't got no sweets on anyone, son, and don't intend on having any. Got enough trouble just runnin' a ranch and stage stop. Don't need woman trouble too," he almost snarled.

Reb chuckled and called to Abe Johnson cleaning one of the horse stalls to join them and they walked to the main house. "I don't like this not knowin' what's going on with them damn Indians," Abe said.

"That why you were cleanin' my barn?" Carothers joshed.

"Maybe. I gotta believe them Paiutes ain't gonna stop with burnin' out Hog Mercer. They'll kill him and his filthy brother and then move on to Josh Whitney's place. Mine would be next in line. I got no reason to be here. I need to protect my ranch. It's all I got in the world, Mr. Carothers."

"I know, son. Let's go talk to Jaime and see if he can offer us some wisdom. Keep in mind there would be fifty or so angry Indians coming down on your place and then there would be just you doing the defendin'." The three trooped into the main house to find Jaime Maldonado dressed for riding, stuffing some dry foodstuff into a saddlebag.

"Leavin' us?" Reb asked.

"Worried about those people, Reb. Your ma, Corcoran, Somerset. Ridin' off to talk to Indians looking for blood and scalps. That's got me worried. Want to ride with me? I can't just sit here one more hour, not knowin' what's goin' on."

"Why don't the four of us ride out," Reb Sonnett said. "If ma and them's in trouble, we can help."

That was all that needed to be said and the four men hustled to the barn to get saddled. Ralph Carothers held back and found Sadie in the kitchen. "Help me make up a quick trail pack, Miss Sadie. We'll need some coffee, flour, dried or smoked meat, and beans. The four of us are gonna see if Corcoran and Pappy need some help."

"Oh, dear, Ralph. Please be careful. You're not as young as you think you are sometimes." He scoffed and scowled watching her hustle up a pack. He nodded thanks and carried it out

They were on the trail to the Hog Mercer ranch within ten minutes. "I don't like leaving East Gate Station Miss Sadie alone like that, but I would sure feel like a fool if I found out that your ma needed help and I wasn't there," Carothers said to Reb.

"Sun'll be down in an hour or so," Jaime Maldonado said. "We can make the big dunes and lay over at the old Pony Express stop. Better shoot something, too, cuz all I brought was biscuits and coffee."

"Miss Sadie put together a good little trail pack for us," Carothers said. "That woman drives me nuts with constant carrying on. Her husband just ran off one day and she ended up on the East Gate front porch alone and hungry."

"And wantin' to be Mrs. Carothers," Reb Sonnett laughed. Carothers took that moment to spat some tobacco juice into the wind.

They rode at a steady hard trot, not stopping once, arriving just at dusk at the big sand dunes Pony Express outpost, no longer in use. "I sure did expect to run into that bunch before getting here," Carothers said. "Damn me, I'm gonna feel bad if we're too late."

"We ain't too late," Reb Sonnett snapped. "Don't talk like that. My ma's gonna be fine." His anger told Jaime Maldonado that the young man was worried half to death that things weren't going to be fine. He wanted to say something to the young man and knew that anything he said would just be words flung into the winds.

They had a fire going and were about to start roasting two scrawny, long-legged Jack rabbits when the sound of approaching riders had them dashing for cover, weapons at the ready. Was it an Indian raiding party or was it Terrence Corcoran's party?

CHAPTER NINE

"It will be a long night, Crying Wolf. The younger men have tasted victory over the white man, have a hunger now, it's like a fire in their bellies." Badger, despite his age, felt the same way. He was a trusted aid to the headman but had a deep hatred for the white men who had devastated the Paiute ways. "I want to take ten of the best and ride to the Whitney ranch and burn it out.

"That man on his knees, the one begging with crying eyes, was Josh Whitney. He and Hog Mercer are the ones responsible for us not getting our cattle allotments. He and Mercer abducted and terrorized our women. You shot him dead, Crying Wolf. Let me burn his ranch to the ground. Then the white man will know our people will no longer tolerate their ways."

Badger was older than Crying Wolf, had fought the army in the Black Rock Desert, had ridden with the Pitt River tribe of Indians in their Lassen wars, and had seen the remains of the desert lake massacre alongside Crying

Wolf. "This opportunity has been a long time coming. We must strike fear in the hearts of the whites."

"We have, my friend. We have. No. There is no need for more blood to flow, no need for more destruction. We have sent the message. We need to see to it that our young warriors know they have struck fear in the whites. They must be made aware that they have done something that was needed to be done, and they did it well."

Crying Wolf looked into his long time friend's eyes and saw that Badger did not agree and turned to Sings Like an Elk. "Join the young warriors, Sings Like an Elk. Let them understand what they have done. We cannot let this become a general war. We have made our point, sent our message." He was a strong leader but could feel the binding strings begin to loosen. The young men didn't want to hear what the elders preached.

Badger and Sings Like an Elk walked off from Crying Wolf's fire to where the drums were beating their call to dance. "He is wrong." Badger was angry and turned from his friend to join a group of young men. In his heart Badger was calling Crying Wolf soft, not being responsible to the people. "He's afraid of the army, Sings Like an Elk. He's afraid we won't stand up to them. I'm ashamed of the man."

Sings Like an Elk shook his head, wondering if Badger would really go against the headman's wishes. Crying Wolf was filled with good medicine and he, Sings Like an Elk must pass that on to the younger warriors. Unlike Badger, this was his first fight.

Badger had eight men sitting around him at his fire. They were eating roasted Mercer beef, laughing and joking about how they had struck fast and hard, winning their first battle against the white man. "We must continue, Badger." It was Long Wings, born into one of the leading families of the tribe and destined to be a leader of the Paiute nation.

"The drums will feed our energy all night, my friends," Badger said. "We will make our way to the horses when it is late, and ride quietly out of this camp. Tell no one or Crying Wolf will surely try to stop us. Today's fight was just the beginning. Tomorrow, Josh Whitney's ranch will be ashes, and then another and another until the white man no longer lives in our lands." His passion was carried to the younger men and his dancing held the strength of the elders. Yes, he could almost feel that he was

worshipped by those around him.

"There will be a river of blood alongside the Carson River. We will call it the Badger River."

Badger had a fierce look on his face, grizzled, angry, scarred from many fights, and the man smelled blood. Badger remembered a long line of Paiute leaders, Numaga, Winnemucca the young, Old Winnemucca, even Truckee, dating back to the first encounters with white immigrants. Peaceful times existed, but the white man seemed to always to want more. Badger's thoughts rambled through wars and fights, incidents of destruction, and his anger built.

"We will ride out late tonight and fight to the death. Death that is, to the white man."

"Hello the fire. We're peaceful," Pappy Somerset yowled out. "And hungry."

"Yer outta luck, Pappy. Got two scrawny rabbits is all.

Ride on in," Ralph Carothers yelled back. "About time you got here. Hope you're bringing good news. We don't need no bad news."

Pappy led the group in. "What you got there?" Abe Johnson asked, watching Sarah lead a fat steer into the camp.

"Didn't want to shoot it. Indians are already pretty riled and a gunshot might set 'em off," she said. "It's a fat steer from the Whitney ranch, and since there ain't no more Whitneys, we brought it for our supper. You do the honors, Abe, but use a knife, not a gun." She threw him the lead rope and stepped down from her horse.

"Three of you rode out and six of you ride in. Better tell us the story, Terrence." Carothers emptied the coffee pot in what cups were offered and started a new pot. "We got ourselves all worried up and come looking for you."

"Better stay worried up, old man. It ain't over even if Crying Wolf thinks it is," Corcoran said. "I don't suppose anyone thought to bring a little jug."

"You bet I did," Carothers laughed. "Almost forgot the food but remembered the important stuff. Is that the young Hennessy boy? Don't tell me Crying Wolf hit Watson's Station first. The Carson stage hasn't come through yet."

"It ain't comin'. Major Watson run off and joined up with Hog Mercer." Corcoran poured a healthy dose of whiskey in his empty coffee cup. "Brought his women folk along for the fight. He abandoned the station and his horse boys run off, too. Crying Wolf never got within thirty miles of Watson's Station."

It took Abe Johnson half an hour to have that calf's tenderloin roasting on hot coals while Corcoran and Pappy

Somerset told the rest of the story. "Watson was the first to die according to Crying Wolf. He killed the Whitney men and is holding Hog and his brother," Terrence said.

"They ain't a stick standing at that ranch," Pappy chuckled. "Gave us the Watson women. Don't blame 'em for that."

"That's not very kind, Pappy," Sarah said. "Kendra and Sandra don't seem to understand how close to death they were." She stopped talking for a few seconds, looking around the now fairly large gathering. "Maybe how close to death we all are."

"What you're saying," Jaime Maldonado said, "is, it ain't over, the Paiutes are going to rampage their way through this whole valley." He poured some whiskey in his cup and looked at Corcoran. "You agree, Corcoran?"

"I do, and I've got a couple of questions for you, Jaime. I've heard it twice now and need an explanation about the cattle allotment given to the Indians. They say they are being shorted and that Mercer and Watson were involved in the shorting."

"I've been investigating those charges for several months, Terrence. I can't prove it, not yet anyway, but I'm sure that the Indian Agent for western Nevada, Joseph Hatch, is in a conspiracy with Mercer, Watson, and Whitney. It's very involved but cattle are stolen, sold to the government, but only a few of those are distributed to the Indians. Hatch then sells the remaining animals on the open market. The allotment shortage is one of Crying Wolf's and Dancing Pines' biggest complaints to the agency." Maldonado just sat back shaking his head wondering how all this has come about. A peaceful existence between the whites and the Paiutes all shot to hell.

"Crying Wolf called for an end to the hostilities but some of those young men are gonna break free and as Tommy Hennessy put it, the fires of Hades are gonna come down on us. We need to get word to the army at Fort McDermitt."

"Nearest telegraph's at Dayton," Carothers said. "I'll write it out and, Tommy, you take this to your father and then into Dayton."

"Give him a horse with a saddle for this ride," Pappy joked. "You okay with that, son?"

"Yes sir. If Pa ain't home, I'll ride it in as quick as I can. The river road is fast to ride on."

It took just a few minutes to get him a fresh horse and he was on his way. A late night ride on the emigrant trail from the sand dunes Pony Express station to where the Carson River turns to its desert sink was rocky in places and often deep and muddy in others. Once on the road along the river, he would have a fast ride.

"What do we do now, Corcoran?" Sarah Sonnett was lounging against a big rock sipping some coffee. "It's gonna get nasty around here before the army boys can get here. If they come at all."

"From where we are right now, where exactly is the Whitney place? If some of those young warriors break out, I think they would want to burn that place first. They already killed the Whitney men. Are there women or children at that ranch?"

"No, old man Whitney chased his wife off years ago. Only he and his two sons lived there. The Lahontan Valley is a fertile little oasis, Terrence, and Whitney was among the first to settle here. His place is on the river, about ten miles from here."

"My God, we just sent that boy to his death," Terrence said. He jumped to his feet and ran to his horse. "I gotta catch him before he rides into a damn Indian war." He was on his horse and gone in seconds. Those around the fire, not in the conversation looked at Sarah.

"What the hell did you say to that man?" Carothers asked, thinking he was being funny.

"How many people at that ranch?" Long Wings was riding alongside Badger as the warriors made their way cross-country from the Mercer ranch.

"Don't know," Badger said. "They be sleeping. We ride in, kill whoever is there and burn the place to the ground. We use the fire from the main house to roast a calf or two," he laughed. Badger spread the men out wide and started riding in a circle around the empty ranch. With each turn he made the circle a little smaller until he signaled and the men started screaming, shooting rifles and arrows, and finally throwing torches through broken windows and onto the roof.

There was no return fire and Badger moved from the main house to the barns and outbuildings burning everything that was manmade. Even the hoist house over the well was burned down. Frustration from the lack of return fire from any of the buildings was beginning to show on Badger and many of the young men. They came to fight and there was no one home.

They came to fight the white man. Where's the glory in burning down empty buildings? They took their frustration out on anything and everything that stood for White Man. Cattle were mutilated, chickens were ripped to pieces, hogs were attacked with knives, stone clubs, lances, and rifles. Blood flowed freely but it wasn't blood from a white man.

"Get the men ready to ride to the Frankmore ranch, Long Wings. Abe Johnson will try to fight back and we will kill him slowly, make him watch as we burn him out and kill his stock. We ride in ten minutes."

Long Wings rode through the warriors whooping, shouting instructions, and in less than five minutes, Badger led the group out and away from the Whitney ranch. The night was black, no moon and heavy clouds covered most of the stars. A wind picked up before sunset and was increasing in intensity as the hours passed.

Tommy Hennessy was riding hard through the night on the well used Carson Road. He passed the rocky Grimes Point and several miles farther out saw the flaming Whitney ranch. He pulled his strong East Gate ranch horse to a stop trying to figure out exactly what he was seeing and the answer came too quick. "Indians," he gasped. He heard Mrs. Sonnett and Mr. Corcoran talking about them coming to burn the ranches and knew he was about to ride into a raiding party. The emigrant road came within half a mile of the main house and he knew he would be seen.

"I've got to get this message to Pa. How can I do that?" He was brought up to understand responsibility, knew those people back there depended on him to get the message through, and also was terrorized to know those Indians would kill him on sight.

Before he could make his mind up he heard the howling Indians racing down the emigrant road, obviously riding hard to Abe Johnson's place. Tommy turned the horse and put it in a furious gallop back toward the group at the dunes. The warriors would turn south toward Johnson's in three miles and he had to be past that turn-off before they spotted him.

His horse was fast but not faster than the Indian ponies and he could hear the war party gaining on him. "Faster, boy. Come on," he yelled at the horse digging his heels into its ribs. "Run, boy, run," he howled over and over. He was fourteen, alone, and more frightened than he had ever been in his short life. Tears streamed across his face and he could hear the screams driving terror deep into him. The wind was strong and he was riding against it. He could feel that horse tiring, straining to go faster.

Tommy Hennessy laid out as low on the horse's neck as he could get, yelling at the top of his lungs for more speed. The Indians spotted him, he could hear the savage cries go up when they did, and terror put its grip on the boy. "Faster, horse, faster," he cried as the screaming horde got closer and closer.

He was half a mile from the turn off to Abe Johnson's ranch but knew the Indians would follow him instead of making the turn. He tried to remember the lay of the land. He had been over this road so many times, riding on the coaches when his father drove. He knew there were big rock formations near the Grimes Point turn off and planned to jump from the horse and try to hide. He made a vow to himself at that moment to never ever be on the back of a horse going anywhere without a firearm, no matter what his mother had to say about it.

He knew the rocks were close but the night was too dark to see well. The wind was blowing dust and sand everywhere, the Indians were almost on him when another rider came alongside out of nowhere. "Follow me, Tommy," Corcoran yelled, and turned north about fifteen yards and pulled his horse to stop behind a large rock formation.

"Jump, Tommy," he said, grabbing the boy in midair and diving to the ground. "Can you shoot?"

"Damn right I can," the boy hollered.

The road split at Grimes point, the emigrant trail continuing east, a road led to Abe Johnson's south, and another angled north, around the point and into empty desert. The two huddled in rocks almost at the point and could hear the war party charging down on them. "Are we gonna die?" he asked, shaking all over. The wind was getting stronger, cold was eating into his strength, and fear boiled his blood.

Corcoran handed the boy his big Colt. "It's loaded and ready. Pick your target, don't just be shootin'. And, no, son, we ain't gonna die."

"That's what Pa always says, too."

Corcoran had to smile, had his Winchester out, and the two were as flat to the ground as possible. Fear boiled through the boy but he was not going to let it keep him from fighting as nine bloodthirsty Paiutes rode down on them. "Slow and steady and pick your target. Let 'em get a little closer, now." The wind was kicking up as much dust as the riders and trying to sight on a single target was difficult.

It was Long Wings riding in front of the party who spotted Tommy, and began the chase. Neither he nor any of the others saw Corcoran come out of the dust and lead Hennessy into the rocks. They had a white man pinned down and their blood ran hot as they fanned out for the kill.

Using hand signals Badger moved the men into a large half-circle around the rocks and began moving them forward. The winds had reached gale force, the dust and sand was thick, and it turned cold. Snow was sure to be falling by sunrise. "This must be Abe Johnson trying to get to his ranch," Badger laughed. "He won't make it."

"They're trying to circle us, Tommy. I don't think they saw me. You protect on the left side, I'll take care of the right. Stay in tight to these rocks and take long careful aim. It's okay to be scared, partner. Gettin' in a fight with Indians is always just a little bit scary."

"I ain't a little bit scared Mr. Corcoran. I'm scared to death."

He heard Tommy try to chuckle but also heard moccasins scraping across rocks in front of where he was crouched down. As Corcoran raised his rifle he heard Hennessy cock the Colt and knew the boy would do fine. "Noisy mocs is about to die," Corcoran whispered, slowly squeezing the trigger, feeling the rifle fire and hearing the scream of death some ten yards in front of him.

Three young, painted, howling braves immediately jumped up and charged where they saw the flash from Corcoran's rifle. He rolled and cocked the Winchester as soon as he fired and shot the first one in line and cocked and was about to take out number two when Tommy Hennessy fired the Colt dropping the man dead.

Corcoran turned to the third man charging and shot him through the chest, rolled again, cocked the rifle and searched for the next target. Young Hennessy had the Colt cocked and was also trying to see something through the dust, and gun smoke. The first drops of cold rain splattered on the rocks around the two.

Corcoran heard the quiet sobs and turned to see Tommy Hennessy wiping his eyes, crying as quietly as he could. Corcoran wrapped his arms around the boy and held him tight. "It's gonna be fine, boy. You did good."

"I ain't never shot nobody. I don't like how I feel, Mr. Corcoran. Mama says it's wrong to kill."

"It is, Tommy, except this is a little different. Those men were trying to kill us and every man has the right to protect himself. If you hadn't shot that man, he would have killed you." He could feel the boy shudder, his crying slowed considerably, but he was shaking.

"They're gonna try again real soon, son. Will you be okay to fight with me against those men who want us dead?"

Tommy moved back a bit from the big arms that held him, wiped the tears away and nodded. "I can fight with you. I know my pa would want me too."

Neither Badger nor Long Wings had expected that kind of return fire from who they thought was one of the valley ranchers. Badger started out with eight braves and now there were only six, including himself. He motioned the men back and sat down under a sage. "There is more than one man in those rocks. We may have ridden into a trap. We'll spread out wide and come in all at once and finish them off."

"Here's what we do, now, Tommy. They think we're here, but let's move back about twenty yards, carefully, quietly, and get behind those big pillars. It will put us about ten feet above them, too."

The wind was strong and carried cold rain now, coming

down in sheets. Neither one of them had slickers or even jackets and huddled in the rocks trying to stay out of the wind.

Corcoran led the youngster, both slowly scrambling through rocks and brush up a steep embankment to hide behind a stand of tall rocks. With the wind whipping through the rocks and brush they didn't worry too much about making noise. "They'll attack where we were, boy. That was good shooting, son."

"Thank you. Pa taught me even though Ma don't want me to have a gun."

"I think she will when we tell her about tonight's fight." He chuckled some and watched through the dust. Even with the heavy rain he could discern Badger spread his small band out. The rain knocked down the dust and he could see the movement of men below him. It was starting to lighten some in the east, the wind was still howling, and the rain was cold enough to have ice crystals in it. "They're gonna rush that spot where we were, Tommy. Are you fully reloaded?"

"I am, sir. I don't know where you came from but I'm sure glad you did."

"Me, too, pal." He looked over to see that Tommy had been crying a little more after their first fight. "It's a little scary but we're gonna win this one. Get ready now, they're about to hit."

CHAPTER TEN

"What the hell's goin' on? Where's he goin'?" Pappy was standing near the fire when Corcoran ran to the horses and rode off.

"He sent the Hennessy kid back to Watson's Station not knowing he had to ride near the Whitney ranch," Sarah said.

"My God, that man's gonna need help. Stay with these women, Sarah. Reb, protect your ma and the women. Abe, Jaime, Ralph, let's ride. Corcoran's riding into an Indian war for sure." Saddles flew through the air, bridles were fastened, and men were sinking spurs in minutes. Pappy spent the first couple of minutes howling at the others, trying to tell them what had happened.

"I know this road better than anyone," Ralph Carothers said. From the sand dunes and Pony Express stop, they had to ride around a large salt marsh through rocky hillside country to Grimes Point where the land flattened into the better part of the Lahontan Valley. "The

Whitney Ranch is a couple or three miles west of Grimes Point."

"My ranch is south of there," Abe Johnson said. "I hope we're in time." It was a hard ride on the rocky trail but they kept their animals at a fast trot eating up the miles. As they rode the storm got stronger, wind whistling its song of destruction, carrying heavy loads of sand and dust. As the night wore on the air became frigid and filled with icy rain.

They topped a rocky ridge and dropped down onto flatter ground picking up some speed. "That sounded an awful lot like gunfire," Pappy said. He was pointing slightly to his right. "Over there," he said. "Where that ridge comes down to the valley floor."

They rode hard knowing that Corcoran and the Hennessy boy were facing an Indian war party that had already tasted blood. They were still half a mile from the point when a second round of shots echoed through the blasting winds and rain. "Hurry," Pappy bawled, all the horses racing at a full gallop. Within seconds it was quiet, no more gunshots.

As the group got within rifle range of the rocks they slowed to a walk, everyone had a weapon cocked and ready, and were as watchful as a hungry owl on a moonlit night. "Too damn quiet," Pappy whispered. The distance between them and the rocks narrowed and finally Pappy couldn't hold it in.

"Corcoran," he howled. "You out there?"

"About time you showed up. We could have used a little help, you know."

The four men rode up to where Corcoran and the boy were standing. Terrence had his arm around the boy who was standing tall holding that big Colt at his side. "We were about to check and make sure all these fools are dead. Nothing worse than a wounded Indian looking to get his last licks in."

"I'll be fine, Reb. If you want to join Ralph and the others." She and Reb stood near the fire listening to the retreating hoof beats from the men riding to help Corcoran. She saw something in his eyes, his face, that told her he wanted to go.

"No, Mama, it's important that I stay and keep you and the Watson women safe. There are marauding Indians out there somewhere and maybe between the two of us we will all be safe."

"You've grown into a fine man, Reb. It's late, son. Kendra and Sandra are asleep and I'm very tired. When you get tired, wake me so you can get some sleep."

"Move your robe over by that downed tree, away from the fire. If we are visited, we don't want to be huddled by the fire just waiting to be shot," he chuckled. He helped her get settled, stoked up the fire a bit, poured some coffee, and melted into the shadows to wait for whatever might happen.

He was surprised when Sandra slipped onto the ground next to him. "Thought you were asleep."

"Can't. I'm so scared, Reb. Are we gonna die?"

"There'll be a heck of a fight first. Why did your father join up with Hog? When I talked to him he shucked me off like bad corn. Said there wouldn't be any Indian trouble."

"I don't know," she whimpered. "They just threw the

dead Whitney boys and pa into the burning buildings. Why are they doing this?"

"Because Mercer kidnapped, raped, and tried to kill one of their little girls, Sandra. Hog Mercer was a vile man and what he did is probably gonna bring on a big war, probably get a bunch more people killed. And your father went to his aid."

"What does your mother think of all this?"

"She ain't said nothing. As long as I can remember, she has always said, 'whatever the Major wants, I'll do it.' She has never talked back to him, never questioned anything he's said or done. He said pack and go, we went."

"Well, he's managed to get us all in a fine mess now. Watson's Station is sitting empty, horses not being tended, and people not being protected."

"You can't blame all this on my father," she said. Her anger was always simmering just below the surface.

"Not all that's happened so far, no. Most of this is on Hog Mercer. But Major Watson should be leading the defense of your station right now. Where do you suppose those Indians will be heading after they burn out Whitney's place? He should have sent a rider to Dayton to telegraph the army, not run off to defend the man responsible for the uprising."

Reb Sonnett had a temper as well and Sandra sat staring at him, slowly letting her anger melt away. Tears followed, but no answers. "What's gonna happen to us, Reb?"

"For the time being, we're safe. That wind is really kicking up, Sandra. It'll be raining soon. Better get you and your mother covered up best as possible. We'll know more when Carothers and them return."

"If they return," she said.

"I remember this one, Terrence," Pappy Somerset said, pointing at Badger's body. "He was the angry one standing with Crying Wolf at his fire. I wonder if more than one group broke off from Crying Wolf's war party."

"That's been bothering me since we left that camp, Pappy. The warriors were gathering around their fires in groups. This one was called Badger, I remember that, and he had several men at his fire as we rode out. How many other little groups were there?"

"You said it as we were leaving, Terrence. You said Crying Wolf couldn't hold them in, couldn't control them now that they tasted blood."

"It's just human nature, Pappy. You've seen it in the army when the fight goes their way, the blood gets hot, and the officers can't control the troops. It becomes a slaughter instead of a battle. These young warriors won't stop despite the pleas from their elders and leaders."

"We need to get back to Sarah Sonnett, Terrence. We left her with the Watson women and Reb."

Corcoran gathered everyone around him. "We still need to get that message off to Fort McDermott. Tommy, you've done more tonight than most men twice your age have done in a lifetime. Are you up to finishing this ride?" Tommy's tear stained face also featured a strong jaw and determined set to his mouth as he nodded. He was wrapped in a duster two sizes too big for him and the rain dripped from his somewhat forlorn hat pulled down snug.

"Good. Still have the message Ralph wrote out? Good. Don't stay on the road, go cross-country to the station, then on to Dayton and the telegraph. With this storm helping keep you from being heard, you should be able to ride fairly fast."

The boy threw his arms around Corcoran, stood back and looked deep into the big man's eyes, turned and jumped on his horse and was gone fast. "That boy just might be Nevada's governor some day," Corcoran chuckled. "Let's ride."

CHAPTER ELEVEN

Walks So Soft led the two other Paiute braves from the now sleeping camp, through the warm ashes of the Mercer ranch, across a low ridge, and into the deep night of the Lahontan Valley. "We ride straight for East Gate and burn that place to the ground. Kill that old man and steal horses." Nobody argued, still feeling the effects of the Mercer ranch raid.

There's something about a young man's first taste of a real fight, when blood flows, screams of death echo through the air, and the stench of the attack lingers on the evening's breeze, particularly when that young man was raised in a warrior society. Those young men were schooled as warriors but hadn't been in a real fight, and now, everything they had heard from the old men, was theirs.

Walks So Soft was eighteen, Kills Birds one year younger, while Yellow Dog was the elder at twenty. None had been on the warpath before, none had fired at a man in anger before, and ironically, not one of them killed anyone during the

Mercer rampage. Runs With the Wind had eyes for Walks So Soft and the two had spent many hours together before Hog Mercer kidnapped the girl. His fight wasn't for past wrongs, it had much more to do with desire for a young girl.

"Crying Wolf's heart is wrong. All the whites are responsible for what happened to Runs With the Wind. They take our hunting lands, they cut our pine nut trees for firewood, they kidnap and use our women and the old men say we would be wrong to seek revenge."

"We are not wrong, Walks So Soft." Yellow Dog was older but not wiser, was always a follower, but was the better hunter of the three. "We will do what the old men should have done many years ago."

"You said East Gate," Kills Birds said. "Why not Watson's Station? That Major Watson always stole from us and was in the barn when we burned it. Crying Wolf let his women go with that man wearing a badge. I say we should burn Watson's Station first. Let the whites know our hatred. Let us taste revenge."

"That man with the badge had the sheep woman with him and I heard him say Carothers was waiting for them. They are headed for East Gate and so are we." Walks So Soft was the leader and the other two fell in behind as he rode toward the emigrant road and the ride to East Gate.

The night was cold, clouds were gathering and the wind was building toward a sure storm as they travelled through the open range. With the others, they had feasted on one of Mercer's fat steers and were content to simply ride their horses at a comfortable pace. "We should find shelter and wait for morning," Yellow Dog said. "The rain will begin soon and I can taste snow in the wind."

"I want to be as close to East Gate as possible by sunrise," Walks So Soft said. "We can make shelter at the great sand dunes and listen to the singing sand. Big medicine in that sand, Yellow Dog."

"They call the singing that of a great spirit from our beginning," Kills Birds said. "Grandmother has gathered pine nuts and listened to the singing. Always late at night, she says."

"I hope the spirits sing for us," Yellow Dog said. The ride through the valley brought them to the emigrant trail and into heavy rain driven by strong winds. It was a far slower ride than Walks So Soft was hoping for and they were still ten miles from the sand dunes when they turned east on the main road.

With Tommy Hennessy riding hard for Watson's Station, Terrence Corcoran got everyone back in the saddle for the ride back to where Sarah Sonnett was keeping care of the Watson women. "That may not be the only raiding party out," Corcoran said. "Let's not just ride headlong into another one. We'll gather up the women and ride straight to East Gate."

"If that Hennessy boy gets through and gets a wire off to the army, and if they actually respond, it will still be three days before we see them," Pappy Somerset snorted. "They should never have left Fort Churchill."

"There hasn't been any Indian problems around here for years, Pappy." Ralph Carothers couldn't remember the last time there had been any kind of incident. "It was Hog Mercer brought all this on, not the Paiutes. God help that man right now, though. They'll have him in little pieces before he finally dies."

"Wouldn't wish that on nobody," Pappy said. The rain had more ice in it than water and wind drove those frozen chunks into the men's faces, clung to their great coats and chaps, and forced the horses to keep their heads low as they made the long slow ride back to the former Pony Express station at the sand dunes. "I sure do like the spring weather, anyway," the old scout said, laughing loud.

It was a combination of the first Paiute War and the Pony Express that created the need for Fort Churchill back then. Virginia City was growing by thousands of people a week, immigrant wagon trains still streamed through Paiute country, and Pony Express riders galloped through Nevada Territory hell bent for leather. Then came civilization and it seemed to crowd out the need for an army fort and Churchill was abandoned.

The road climbed up into the rocky slopes above the salt flats and then went level along the hillside for a good seven or eight miles. The group had just topped that little climb when Pappy called out for a halt. He jumped down from this horse and almost got down onto his knees.

"Whatcha got, Pappy?" Corcoran stepped off Rube and knelt down next to the old tracker.

"Three horses, Terrence. See? Looks like they rode in from the general direction of the Mercer ranch down that way. They had to skirt around the salt flats and came up onto the road from a western angle. Terrence, they are riding toward where Sarah Sonnett is right now. They ain't white men riding' them horses, Corcoran."

"Those tracks must be fresh the way the wind and snow is blowing. Let's ride," Corcoran snapped.

. . .

Walks So Soft threw his arm up halting the three. "Smoke, Kills Birds. Smell it?" The three Indians had their faces moving about, sniffing, trying to locate where the smoke was coming from. The wind was still raging, driving a combination of rain and snow into their faces, making the job difficult.

"Straight ahead, where the road climbs out of the valley. We will make our first kill at that fire." Kills Birds had his blood up and hot and wanted to ride fast into the camp and kill everyone there.

"No, we will ride quiet and slow. There might be ten men there with guns, Kills Birds. We ride slow, find out who is there, then kill them." He kicked his horse back into a trot knowing the storm would hide any noise they might make. They covered the last mile quickly, dismounting several hundred yards from the old station, now surrounded by overgrown cottonwood and aspen. Walks So Soft told the men to stay in sight of each other and sent Yellow Boy to the left and Kills Birds to the right. He advanced quietly on the camp.

The fire was burning good despite the rain and wind but no one was sitting or standing near it. Walk So Soft settled low behind a stand of brush and watched for several minutes before spotting Reb Sonnett crouched in a patch of young aspen. He then spied Sarah Sonnett and the two Watson women huddled near some fallen cottonwood.

He caught Yellow Dog's eye and motioned to the women. Kills Birds was already advancing on Reb and Walks So Soft held back to be able to move to either side for help if needed. Yellow Dog was clumsy moving through the wet brush and Sarah picked up the movement immediately. She didn't hesitate a second, raised her rifle and fired into the brush twice.

The Winchester was cocked for a third shot when the lights went out. Walks So Soft had run up behind her and laid her flat with the butt of his rifle to the back of her head. The gunfire had Sandra Watson wide-awake and she was screaming hysterically when Walks So Softly knocked her unconscious, again with the rifle butt.

Kendra Watson awoke in time to see Sandra's bloody body fall into the mud next to her. Her screams were stopped with a moccasin driven into her mouth followed by a rifle barrel across her forehead.

Reb was on his feet and running toward the screaming when he spotted Kills Birds advancing on him, rifle pulled to his shoulder. Reb spun, fell to the ground, and fired his revolver twice, killing Kills Birds. He scrambled into a stand of aspen and saw Walks So Soft kill Kendra Watson and turn to Sandra.

Reb raised the pistol and slowly squeezed a round off. The bullet hit a tree twig and ruined the shot. Walks So Soft spun and fired his rifle from the hip, driving a slug deep into Reb's left leg. He went down in screaming pain, rolled into a stand of trees and burrowed as close to the ground as he could get. Blood was pumping from the wound and he ripped his bandanna off and tied it tight to the wound, stemming the blood for the moment.

Weakness set in immediately and Reb was still trying to get his wound tied up when he passed out. Walks So Soft was about to slash Sandra Watson's throat when he heard moaning from the bushes nearby. He flung her helpless body to the ground and rushed into the bushes where Yellow Boy was huddled, a bullet wound pumping blood from his chest into the mud. When he tried to talk, pink blood splattered from his mouth and Walks So Soft knew the man would die in minutes.

Walks So Soft was alone in a white man's camp. The white man was wounded or dead, and two women were alive. There was no panic, but his anxiety level was considerable as he sifted through his options. He could simply ride off, return to Pyramid Lake and tell of his raid, or he could capture a white woman. He chose the second.

Sandra Watson, unlike her more than hefty mother, was a thin fifteen-year-old, and the big Paiute held her by one arm as he mounted his horse. He planned to trail the other two horses but in the process of moving off, one was left behind. He made for the hills north of the big dunes knowing that once he crossed, they would drop into a long flat valley that would take him north to the Humboldt Sink and home.

"Trouble!" Corcoran bellowed the word at the first sound of muted gunfire coming from where their camp should be. He kicked Rube hard and was at full gallop, Pappy, Ralph, and Jaime right behind. Wet snow blowing in gale winds hampered the mile ride in, and Corcoran jumped from the still sliding Rube, rifle in hand when he spotted the bloody body of Kendra Watson splayed across the rocks.

"My God, they beat that woman to death," he growled, trying to look in every direction at the same time. His rifle was at the ready and he took only two steps when he saw Sarah Sonnett crouched alongside a large rock.

"She's alive," he hollered, racing to her side. She wasn't fully conscious yet and tried to fend him off when he eased her up out of the mud and snow. "Easy now, Sarah. It's Corcoran here. You've taken a couple of nasty knocks, old girl." She responded to his soft murmurs and gentle hands and slowly came to, her arms wrapped tightly around his burly neck.

Pappy and Jaime were searching for Sandra and Reb and spotted blood on the trunk of an aspen tree. Pushing deeper into the stand they found Reb. "Got Reb, Corcoran. He's shot bad but he's alive."

Ralph Carothers followed some bloody drag marks that ended where horses had been picketed. "I think Sandra's been taken, Terrence. I found one dead Indian, but at least two seem to have ridden off with someone who was bleeding heavily."

"Yeah, I just found another dead one over here," Jaime called out, "Lung shot and bled out. I'll get that fire burning good and we better be ready for another attack."

Reb's leg wound was bad in itself but the young man also lost considerable blood and was in and out of consciousness. Sarah's head wound was serious and was still bleeding as she was moved near the fire.

"We're in a hell of a mess," Corcoran said quietly as he poured fresh coffee and passed the big pot to Pappy. "These two need lots of attention and we have a young girl that's been abducted. Jaime, your job requires that you get to the nearest telegraph station and alert your superiors to what's happened. You need to ride fast and hard."

"I know, Terrence. I hate to leave you, but the Bureau

of Indian Affairs needs to know about this right now. Hopefully the Hennessy boy gets his messages through, but I need to inform Major McPherson and Agent Hatch. This could turn nasty and bloody. But these people need help. Damn."

"That Watson girl needs help, too. Pappy, you and I need to be on that trail in the next ten minutes while we can still see it. It will be buried under snow in less than an hour."

"I'll just stay right here, Terrence. It won't be the first time I've taken care of the wounded in some damn fool out of the way camp. I've got plenty of guns and ammo, still have food and coffee, so go. Reb is hurt bad but Abe and I can take on the whole damn tribe if we have to. Go find Sandra Watson before she is destroyed by those savages."

Jaime Maldonado stuffed some of the roasted beef and coffee into his saddlebags and was off in minutes. Corcoran and Somerset stuffed raw meat and coffee in theirs, bid Ralph, Abe, and Reb goodbye. Corcoran bent down next to Sarah and gave her a little pat on the head. "We'll be back," is all he said, jumped on Rube, and rode off.

They found the horse Walks So Soft let get away and brought him along. "Solid trail to follow, Terrence. Looks like they're headed straight north, probably not figuring on being followed.

"The wind is actually doing us a favor, keeping the snow from piling up. It'll drift some, but there will be large open areas where those hoof prints will stand out in the mud."

It was bitter cold with near white-out conditions. The

wind was whipping and coming from the four points of the compass, snow cascading in waves on the two, and the trail slowly disappearing. This was going to strain even the abilities of Pappy Somerset's at following a trail.

"I'm not sure it's two, Pappy. It looks more like one rider trailing a horse. We might be following just one man holding a wounded girl and trailing a horse. That will surely slow him down."

"Yup," is all Pappy said. They followed along the western edge of a mountain range and across a wide, marshy plain. "He knows this country well, Corcoran. To our west is the Carson Sink and north of us is the Humboldt Sink. He'll thread his way through that and head toward where the Truckee River turns north to the big lake."

The wind continued blowing hard, driving snow mixed with rain, and obliterating the tracks they were following. Pappy found himself going for long stretches without seeing prints and hoping the Indian didn't make a turn. "We find that boy, Corcoran, I'm gonna rip his heart out."

"Only if you get to him before I do," Corcoran chuckled. "I could sure use a mug full of hot coffee laced with some fine brandy about now."

"You need to sit and rest, Sarah. You took a solid thump to that pretty head of yours and trying to do everything that needs to be done is gonna knock you out. Let me take care of you and Reb. Abe is getting wood for the fire, taking care of the food, and making sure we aren't gonna get attacked again."

"You're the kindest man, Ralph. Are you really giving

up the stage stop? I thought you loved having that and all the people that come through."

"I did, but I'm getting older and it's far more work than I want to do. I still have my ranch to run. Them cattle need me too, just as yours need you. I've got good grass and plenty of water pouring out of the Desatoya Mountains, and my herd is growing."

"All these years, Ralph, and you've never married." She had a little smile on her bruised face and wanted to say so much more to Carothers. She never understood why the man didn't come calling when her husband was killed. Even Reb, much younger then, of course, commented on it.

"I'm a little too cantankerous for most of the women I've met, and I hate being catered to. Miss Daisy drives me nuts. Always wantin' to know if I want something, or more of something I already have. I can take care of myself," he snorted and got up to find more wood for the fire. Sarah Sonnett had to smile through the pain she was feeling.

CHAPTER TWELVE

"Pa! Pa!" Tommy Hennessy was yelling at the top of his lungs as he rode hard into Watson's Station. The young man jumped from the still running horse and raced to the clapboard cabin along the banks of the Carson River.

"Whoa down there, boy. Slow up now," Hennessy said, catching the boy as he hurtled onto the porch. "You been shot, boy? That your blood?"

"No, no, Pa, me and Mr. Corcoran got in a fight with some Indians. We gotta get to Dayton and send a telegram to the army. Hurry, Pa."

"I'm sure you think you know what you're talking about, but I don't. You sit down here, calm down, and start from the beginning. I sent you to East Gate Station, Then what?"

Tommy Hennessy had a quick mind, knew he had to make his father understand what had happened, caught his breath, and plopped down in a chair on the porch. He had the whole story out, questions were asked, and Pa Hennessy knew he had to ride with his son to Dayton.

"That's an incredible story, Tommy," his father said. "Looking at you, I have to believe every word of it. I can get a rescue posse organized when we get to Dayton. We'll need to send wires to the Nevada First Volunteers in Carson City as well. That fool Hog Mercer just couldn't keep his pants on."

Hennessy ran across the large compound to find Standish Pearl, one of the best coach messengers on the line. His shotgun had ended more than one attempted hold up. Hennessy needed him to guard the compound, the families, and prepare them for a possible raid while he and Tommy made the ride to Dayton.

Hennessy knew that he would have to get the people living at or near Watson's Station out of there as soon as the telegrams were sent. "What them damn Indians are doing ain't right either, but I know why they're so fired angry." Hennessy rode with the army as a scout during the Second Paiute War and knew just how savagely the Paiutes could fight.

"Make sure these people understand the seriousness, Mr. Pearl. They need to be packed and ready to move when we get back. Keep the horses in a tight corral and be ready for anything. Damn that Major Watson, but what Tommy told me, he's having a hot old time down below right now." Pearl was still laughing as Hennessy and his son rode out of the station.

The road to Dayton was a good one, mostly level all the way in, and the two kept their horses at a solid trot with one brief slow down to let them catch their breath. They reined up at the stage stop and Hennessy dashed inside leaving Tommy to take care of the horses.

"Better get that telegraph heated up, Elmo. We got us

a problem," Hennessy said stepping into the alcove used by the operator. When the telegraph lines were laid out the stage line contracted as operators. The telegraph drove the Pony Express out of business before the railroads could, and was not helping the bottom line for mail carriers.

"Indians attacked the Mercer place, burned it out, and have burned out the Whitney ranch. We need to hold the stages that are coming in from both directions and send an alert to the army in Fort McDermott."

"I been afraid of this ever since the last time that fool Mercer took a young Indian girl. We need some damn law out there in that valley, Hennessy. You've been held up twice this year and ain't nobody done nothing. They talk about county this and county that but ain't no man waling around with a star pinned to his chest."

There was no organized community in the Lahontan Valley, no county sheriff with deputies, no justice court, and that allowed the likes of Hog Mercer, Major Watson, and Joshua Whitney to do as they pleased. It was Hog Mercer's carnal desires that brought the issues to a head.

"I'm heading back to take care of the Watson's Station people as soon as those wires are out," Hennessy said. "There's people at East Gate that need help, too. Those ranchers out there are on their own, I'm afraid unless old man Carothers gathered them in."

It's a long stretch of open range from Dayton to Austin. There were several lush valleys on that stretch and several areas that truly qualified as desert. The one thing missing was any organized community, thus no organized law.

Elmo Butters was furiously tapping out messages as he

spoke. "This long road across to Austin and east ain't got no protection since the army pulled out. What about Watson's Station? Burned out?"

"No, they didn't attack the station. Major Watson went to Hog Mercer's aid for some damn reason and abandoned the station. Can't do nothing about that, though. He's dead. I gotta get back, Elmo. My wife and two other drivers and their families are there alone. I'll get everyone moving back this way."

"The company will send men from Carson City, Hennessy, and I'll put together a few from here and come to Watson's Station just as quick as we can. Go protect those people there. You'll have help."

Pa Hennessy found Tommy still holding the horses and the two were in the saddle and on the way home. "I need to get back to the station, son. You're about the only fourteen year old man I've ever rode with." Hennessy was chuckling, whacked his son across the shoulders, and got a good laugh from the boy. "I want you to ride to Aunt Bessie's in Virginia City. I'll bring your ma and the others quick as I can."

"No, Pa," Tommy said. "You can't do all that alone and you said I been acting like a real man. You need my help. Ma needs us."

Hennessy sat very still in his saddle, looking deep into his son's eyes. "For fourteen years you're somethin', boy. We'll spread the word to those that live along the Carson River and bring everyone from the station back here. Let's go."

They stopped at half a dozen small operations along the river spreading the word about the Paiute uprising. Hennessy was surprised to find many not really believing that they might be in danger. All he could do was shake his head and ride hard to the next ranch.

"We're riding straight for the Truckee River, which will take us right smack into the Pyramid Lake Indian village, Corcoran. Unless you've got some kind of plan tucked away in that miserable sombrero you wear, we need to hold up."

"I know, Pappy. I know. I was really hoping we would catch up with whoever it is carrying that Watson girl. The last time I was through here the Paiutes were a friendly bunch. Let's stay on this man's trail just as long as we dare, Pappy."

"I see something twisting around in that head of yours. Give it some fresh air, Terrence."

Corcoran had to chuckle at his old friends comments. "You got a way about you. But, yeah, I am thinking that we gotta know just what's going on with Crying Wolf and the rest of the tribe. I don't think he's gonna be happy when one of his warriors rides into the village with a white girl hostage.

"It was a young girl being held for hostage that started all this mess. Let's keep following this fool."

They cleared one more range of mountains before dropping into the lush Truckee River valley where it turns north to Pyramid Lake. "There are some deep cuts that the river has made over the years, Pappy, just in front of us. That's where the Paiutes whipped the hell out of Captain Storey in the first Paiute war. They were a volunteer group. It was the regular army that straightened things out the second time."

"Yeah, Terrence, and we're about to get right in the middle of the third war." Pappy pulled his horse up short, looking off to his right. "You see that?"

"Yup, Let's ride." Corcoran put Rube in a fast run toward a stand of cottonwood trees some fifty yards or so in front of them. Both men were off their horses and Corcoran grabbed up the swatch of cloth hanging on a branch. "That bastard did her right here, Pappy. This is from the bodice of her dress. Let's get off this main trail now and get as close to that village as we can."

Many of the tribal elders had seen Crying Wolf angry in the past but none could remember this level of pure hate from the man as he stood over the unconscious Walks So Soft. The renegade rode right into the village holding the unconscious and almost naked Sandra Watson. He shouted out how he had attacked the group, killed everyone except the girl, and brought his prize back to the village.

Crying Wolf and many of the elders were stunned, and the headman ripped the girl from Walks So Soft and handed her to the women gathered around, He jerked the young warrior from his horse and beat him senseless with his fists. He turned from the bloody heap to the gathered elders. "We meet," he said, and strode toward his wigwam.

The women gathered up the warrior and would hold him until the elders made a decision on what to do with him. They hustled Sandra Watson into a wigwam to tend her wounds. Visions of Runs With the Wind echoed as they worked.

Many of the young warriors who had ridden in the recent raid on Mercer's ranch had tasted blood for the first time but were aware that they were attempting to right a wrong: the abducting and abuse of one of their young women by Hog Mercer and his brother. Now they have been witness to one of their own warriors committing the same exact foul crime against a white girl.

If looks alone told the story, no one supported the actions of Walks So Soft. Many were aware that two others, Kills Birds and Yellow Dog had ridden off with Walks So Soft. Where were they? He lay bleeding in the dirt and sand of the village for more than an hour before the women gathered, put him on a horse and led him from the village. It was hours later they returned with the horse. No questions were asked.

The elders gathered in Crying Wolf's lodge. "Walks So Soft and his followers were not the only ones to ride off from the Mercer raid," Crying Wolf began when the elders were seated around the fire. A pipe was lit and passed about. Every face held the knowledge that what happened was probably the opening round in a war with the white army.

"Badger, my trusted friend, deserted our camp and took several braves with him. Long Wings hasn't been seen since the night of the attack and may have several young men with him. Sings Like an Elk has managed to keep most of our young men with us, but the army will only hear what they want to hear."

"They will hear that the Paiute nation has attacked white ranches, abducted white girls, killed white women, and they will attack. In their minds we have started a war. There will be no talk. They will not hear that Hog Mercer abducted Runs With the Wind, will not hear that we only wanted to punish Mercer and his filthy friends the Whitney's."

"The Indian Bureau lawman knows what we did and why," Shaking Rocks said. "He was here before your raid. Will he speak for us?" Several of the elders nodded at the idea. "Jaime Maldonado has been our friend for some time."

"He has," Crying Wolf said. "He works for that lazy dog Hatch. Joseph Hatch is no friend of the Paiute. He steals what is ours and sells it to others. He lies to his friends in Washington about us." He stopped for a minute in contemplation. "Maybe I will send a rider to Carson City to find Maldonado."

"Send someone who talks white man. Maldonado does not talk Paiute very good. Angry Bear talks good white talk. He worked for white man in Virginia City." Shaking Rocks remembered too that Angry Bear used to dress like a white man. "He can wear white man clothes and ride to Carson City safely."

The meeting lasted for another half hour and everyone agreed with the plan. Crying Wolf sent for Angry Bear and told him everything that had happened and outlined what the elders wanted him to do.

"I will talk with Maldonado. I know him. We have hunted together. But I won't talk with Hatch. He is bastard. That what Maldonado says, not me. I will do as you ask because it is the right thing to do. Walks So Soft should die, Crying Wolf." Crying Wolf and the elders simply nodded, more than one with a slight smile.

Angry Bear rode from the lakeside village an hour later to the great enjoyment of those around. Dressed in black wool pants, unbuttoned white shirt minus its collar, and a red wool waistcoat, he did not look like your typical white man. He did sport a bowler type hat set square on his always-angry looking head, his long black hair streaming out in every direction. He did not smile despite all the laughter and creative epithets hurled his way, but rode straight and proud on his war pony.

"We need to prepare the people for what will happen," Shaking Rocks said to Crying Wolf as Angry Bear passed their lodge. "The army could be here in three days or less."

Crying Wolf remembered the last time the army came to the village. It was in the dry desert lake to the east, and few lived through the day. He knew that Sarah Winnemucca spoke white talk and told about the massacre. "We should tell the people to melt into the desert, go find pine nuts, gather grasses, make willow baskets anywhere but here."

This had been done before when the tribe was threatened. The people would scatter into the desert in small family groups and stay out of sight of any and all white men. They had lived in this high mountain plateau the white men called Nevada since the beginning of time and knew they could survive.

"What do we do with the white woman?" Shaking Rocks knew she would be in the minds of every white man. "She must be protected."

"She will be with my family. Runs With the Wind will see to it that she is cared for," Crying Wolf said.

The dispersal began immediately after the deaths of Hog Mercer and his brother. The women saw to it that they died at about the same time. There was no greater fear among white men on the frontier than being captured and then tortured by the women of the tribes and villages.

. . .

"That Indian bastard is still several hours ahead of us, Terrence. Let's move off this trail and settle in somewhere. We can try to get close to the village after the sun goes down. For all we know there's ten sets of eyes watching us right now."

"I know you're right, Pappy. Hatred certainly has strange ways of making a nuisance of itself, eh? Mercer hates Indians and takes it out on little girls. Paiutes hate white people and take it out on whoever is available. This fool we're following, whoever he is, tried to kill everyone and now takes his hate out on a little white girl."

"It's fear of the unknown, Terrence. I've seen it for many more years than you. It doesn't matter what color you are, white, red, black, yellow, it's the unknown that frightens you, and when you're afraid, it's easy to hate what you fear. We won't take the time or make the effort to learn about what it is we fear. It's better to hate it, kill it, do away with it, than to learn that we don't need to fear it."

"Sometimes I wish I could talk like you, Pappy. And then again, I'm kinda glad I can't." They chuckled as they rode from the ugly scene of Sandra's attack. "Let's find a stand of cottonwoods and hide out some."

They started up out of the deep ravine they were in when Pappy held up his hand. He motioned Corcoran to be quiet and stepped off his horse, handing the reins over. Corcoran stepped down as well and watched Pappy Somerset slowly climb hand over hand up the steep walls of the culvert.

"Damndest thing I've ever seen, Terrence," he said,

sliding back down. "Big Indian dressed in white man's clothes, riding out."

"Think we can catch him?"

"Yup," is all Pappy said.

They walked their horses out of the culvert and mounted for the chase. "He was walking his horse," Pappy said. "We can catch him in the flats where the river turns west." They made their way through high brush and scattered willows along the Truckee River, following the fresh tracks. As they approached a stand of cottonwoods, Angry Bear rode out from behind a large tree.

"I am riding to Carson City to find Indian Agency policeman Maldonado." He pointed at Corcoran and continued in halting English. "You are police too. I see you before when you talk with Crying Wolf. You ride with me."

Angry Bear carried a bow and quiver of arrows but did not brandish his weapon. "Maybe you should tell us why you're riding into the capital," Pappy said.

Angry Bear turned his horse and rode off at a walk, Corcoran and Somerset riding right along with him. The proud, tall Indian spent the next half hour telling them what had happened and what he expected to do in Carson City.

CHAPTER THIRTEEN

"I see smoke, Pa." Tommy Hennessy was pointing east along the Carson River toward where Fort Churchill was and near where Watson's Station should be. The Carson River flows through a long canyon from the plains east of Dayton. There are steep hills on both sides of the river and great stands of cottonwood trees in the canyon. The smoke was about three miles away.

"I'm not sure where you got that rifle but I'm glad you have it," Pa Hennessy said as the two put their horses into a fast run. "We don't want to ride into a horde of Indians, Tommy, so follow my lead. When I slow down, you slow down."

"I will," the boy said. The canyon opened up just before reaching where the soldiers built Fort Churchill, and as they approached what was left of the fort they slowed their ride to a walk. Down river and on the other side lay Watson's Station and the smoke was coming from one of the outbuildings used to maintain equipment.

Hennessy rode slowly across the river toward his home

some way out from the station. Ma Hennessy ran from the house when she saw the two ride up. "Hank, Tommy, my God, I was so worried," she said as she ran from the porch.

"We saw the smoke," he said. "What's happened? Are you all right? Where is everyone?" Questions flew from him, one after the other without waiting for answers.

"Three Indians rode in shooting, but Standish Pearl shot one of them and the other two threw torches into the shed and the barn. Mr. Pearl kept shooting and they rode off. He and Linda and Mr. Smith put out the fire in the barn but couldn't put out the shed fire. Too much stuff to burn in there." She was talking fast, from fear, from trying to get it all out at once.

"Let's get everyone together, Ma. We got to get out of here." In his haste to get the word out was he to blame for this Indian attack? Pa Hennessy wasn't the kind of man to turn his back on his family and friends and this question would bother him for some time to come. He didn't have time to think on it right at the moment.

"Tommy, run from house to house, spread the word to pack only what's necessary and be ready to leave in half an hour. Take your rifle with you." He looked at his wife to see if she was questioning his judgment. "Was I wrong? Should I have stayed and sent Tommy to Dayton?"

"No, Pa, you weren't wrong. You didn't know, no one knew those three would show up. You're lead man at the station, the Major and his women ran off, and you did what had to be done."

Pa Hennessy watched the boy run off, got his wife headed back to the house to pack and ran to meet up with Stan Pearl who was still near the barn. "Got one of 'em, eh?"

"Yeah, Pa, right through the heart, too. Heathen savages." Standish Pearl was nearing thirty, rode shotgun on the line most of the time. He was a crack shot with rifle, pistol, and shotgun. He was short, thick, and strong, with wild light colored hair that cascaded wherever the wind blew it. He never trimmed his beard and only cut his moustache back when it got in the way of his eating habits. "What's the word from Dayton? Army coming?"

"Maybe." Most of the men and women around the station called Hennessy, Pa, even some of those that were older than he. "All the stages have been cancelled until this uprising ends. We need to get everyone out of here and back to Dayton. Major Watson is dead, don't know about Kendra or Sandra. Elmo Butler sent wires to Fort McDermott, Carson City, and the Indian agent, Hatch. I'm not counting on any help."

There were three families, the Hennessy's, Pearl's, and Smith's hustling to get their gear in wagons. The hangers-on split at the first sign of problems. Tommy and Stan Pearl were harnessing horses and moving wagons around for loading when a gunshot rang out and the horse Tommy was working on, screamed out in agony, rearing, then falling. Tommy had to dance out of the way of the flailing hooves as the horse breathed its last.

The boy raced to the barn and grabbed his rifle, diving behind some stacked bales of straw as two more shots were fired. Pearl dove behind the dead horse as bullets dug furrows in the dirt near where he had been standing. He had his pistol out looking about for whoever was shooting.

"You okay, boy?" he shouted.

"I'm fine. Can you see anything? I can't." Tommy was shaking, fighting off the fear of another Indian attack. He wasn't over his first Indian attack and now was in another. He lay in the dirt, biting his lip, making fists, kicking his feet, doing anything to try to calm down, to blot out the terror.

He was looking across the river and saw a puff of smoke, heard the bullet pass close over his head, and then heard the rifle shot. He remembered what that huge deputy sheriff told him about shooting and leveled his rifle, aiming at where that puff of smoke came from. His finger eased its way slowly back, all shaking gone, and felt the kick as the rifle fired.

He didn't hear anything but saw the bushes rustle and then saw an Indian try to run toward some rocks. He was limping from a wound in his side and Tommy took a long steady aim and fired once more. The man went down hard and didn't move.

"Damn fine shooting, son," Pa Hennessy said as he raced into the barn and dropped down next to his boy. "Damn fine."

"That leaves at least one more," Pearl hollered. "There were three of them come riding in. Now, there's at least one more out there somewhere."

"Better to think there's ten of 'em, Stan," Pa Hennessy yelled. He moved deeper into the barn and its shadows. "I'm gonna have a look out the back. Keep an eye on the houses, Stan, make sure nobody goes after the women. Tommy, you keep an eye on that riverbank. We gotta get out of here."

There was no movement, no gunshots or attacks for fifteen minutes and Hennessy decided to take a chance and look around the compound. "Keep my backside safe, you two," he said with a chuckle, walking out of the barn.

It was a quick, cursory look around and when no shots were taken and nothing could be seen or heard, Pa came back into the barn.

"Take care of your ma and the other women, Tommy. Let's see if number three's still around, Mr. Pearl. We'll walk the outer perimeter and shake him out if he's still around."

They made their way around the corrals, working into willows along the river when a fully painted warrior came screaming out of the brush toward them. The young brave was swinging a stone ax when Pa Hennessy dropped him with a single shot through the middle of his chest.

"He isn't much older than Tommy," Standish Pearl said stooping over the sprawled body. "I don't think we should take the time to bury these three. There sure as hell could be more on the way." His flyaway hair was blowing in the wind and his eyes were searching in every direction. Pa Hennessy nodded at the man who had protected him on so many journeys across the state.

Highwaymen feared the name Stan Pearl and it was rare when one of his coaches was held up. He had been with Pa Hennessy when the Pettiford Gang out of Utah hit the stage just west of Austin last year. Four masked men with rifles and pistols appeared from behind large rocks and stopped the stage.

Three bodies and one prisoner were brought into Austin, passengers and mail were safe, and Pa Hennessy bought Stan's supper at the International Hotel that night. All the steak he could eat and beer he could drink.

Smith was also a driver and had the women gathered in the center of the station's big yard. Three wagons were hitched and loaded. "Tommy, you, me, and Mr. Smith will each be in a wagon and Mr. Pearl, you ride shotgun on your horse. Ladies, you drive." It would be a long slow ride back to Dayton. "I'm not sure we'll make it by sundown."

"If what you told us is the truth, Angry Bear, we have to ride hard to Carson City. We might just stop this war before it starts." Corcoran was nudging his horse into a faster trot as he talked. "Damn stupid fools."

"Young men fighting against bad treatment," Angry Bear snapped.

"And in turn are giving out bad treatment," Pappy Somerset snapped back.

"I'm not sure Crying Wolf was right in attacking Hog Mercer's place. On the other hand there isn't any law in this part of the state, so he did the only thing left to him. It's Mercer who was the most stupid of the bunch. The young warriors not listening to the elders are also damn stupid fools."

Angry Bear's eyes spoke for him when he looked away rather than answering. Corcoran grinned and chuckled and put Rube in a faster trot. "How many men didn't return from the raid?" He asked the sullen Angry Bear.

"Maybe fifteen. Maybe more. Don't know. What you thinking, Corcoran?"

"We're fifteen miles or so from the river, making good time, and should be in Dayton before night comes. It's another fifteen miles from there to Carson City but if I light out fast right now, I can make Carson not too long after sunset. Pappy, you and Angry Bear come on in tomorrow."

"We'll skirt around Dayton and stay off the main road, Terrence."

"Good," is all Corcoran said touching Rube with his spurs putting the horse in a strong lope across the broad Nevada desert. Rolling hills held stands of piñon, cedar, and sage along with grasses and rabbit brush. The ground was rocky, some areas of shale along steep hillsides, but Corcoran made good time to the river and the main emigrant trail into Carson City.

"Come on, Rube, that's smoke coming from Watson's Station. Hope we're in time to help them folk." He was less than a mile from the station and rode in hard and fast only to find the station deserted. He found the dead Indians, saw the tracks of several wagons pulling out and was back on the trail in minutes.

At a fast trot, Rube ate up the miles never breaking sweat along the almost flat road that followed the Carson River through the deep canyon. Corcoran spotted dust a mile or so in front and urged Rube on. He caught up with Hennessy and the others in just a few minutes.

Standish Pearl was the first to spot the rider coming up fast from behind them. "Might have some trouble coming, Pa," he hollered. He turned his horse and pulled that rifle from its scabbard, holding a bead on Corcoran coming up fast.

"No," Tommy Hennessy yelled. "That's Corcoran. Don't shoot," he howled. Pearl pulled the rifle down but held it at the ready as Corcoran rode up to the wagons.

"Hello, again, Tommy Hennessy," he shouted, jumping down from Rube. "Which one of these men is your father?"

"I am," Pa Hennessy said from the lead wagon.

"We need to talk," Corcoran said. "I think I might need to steal that boy of yours one more time." He looked over at Tommy. "You up to another fast ride?" It was a nod filled with a big smile that came back Corcoran's way.

The group gathered around Corcoran who spelled out what he knew and what he thought might happen. "Near as we can tell, the Paiute tribe is not on the warpath, have no plans on raiding every ranch in the Lahontan Valley, and we can end the problem if we pull in our horns."

"Spell it out, Corcoran, because we just killed three of those bastards up at the station," Stan Pearl said. The others nodded in agreement.

"There may even be one or two other small groups out in the desert," Corcoran said. "These are renegades acting without the tribe elder's consent. In the whole valley, from Watson's Station to East Gate Station, there might be as many as five renegade warriors and I think that Jaime Maldonado can see to it that Crying Wolf gets them back at the Pyramid Lake village. I need to get word to him just as quickly as I can."

"You want me to ride to Carson City?" Tommy was excited about that idea.

"No, I'm making that ride," Corcoran said. "I would like you to ride to Dayton and get a wire off to Jaime. I know wires were sent to Mr. Hatch, the Indian Agent, but I don't trust that man an inch. Maldonado needs to know what's been going on and to expect me sometime tonight."

Pa Hennessy started to say something but was cut off by Tommy. "I can do it, Pa. I've already been in two Indian fights, ridden half way across Nevada, and I have my own rifle now." He held up the rifle he and Corcoran had taken from Badger back at the Grimes Point fight.

Hennessy had to smile and was shaking his head back and forth slowly thinking what a fine boy he and Ma Hennessy had raised. “Like I said a while back, son, you ain’t a boy no longer. Mr. Pearl would you be kind enough to let my son ride your horse like the devil was on his back into Dayton?”

Pearl jumped from the horse, Tommy jumped from his wagon, and the boy was in the saddle racing for Dayton before Stan Pearl could climb to the wagon’s seat. “He’s one hell of a boy, Mr. Hennessy,” Pearl said.

“You folks have a safe drive,” Corcoran said. He mounted Rube and was off on a fast ride into Carson City, less than thirty miles in front of him.

CHAPTER FOURTEEN

"That Angry Bear feller pointed out each building as we rode into town, Terrence. He lived in Virginia City and worked for one of the businessmen up there. Drove a wagon into Carson City once a month to deliver and pick up merchandise. He's pretty smart if I do have to say so." It didn't set right with the old scout to have to say he made a friendship with an Indian. "I can say I actually enjoyed his company. He got his name right, for sure. Quick to say what's on his mind," he chuckled.

"Sounds like somebody I know," Corcoran chuckled. "Kind of opinionated like."

Pappy Somerset and Corcoran were having breakfast at the St. Charles Hotel while Jaime Maldonado and Angry Bear were planning their return to Pyramid Lake. "More than one person gave him a nod or wave as we came in. What's your plan?"

"We need to get back to the village, we need to make sure Carothers and Sarah Sonnett are okay, we need to get Watson's Station reopened and the coaches back on the road, and we need to call off the army if they have even given thought to responding.

"Other than that, Pappy, I got nothing to do but sit and drink coffee with you." The two men were still laughing as they made their way out of the dining room and across the way to the Indian Agency offices located on the block behind the capitol building.

Two men were lounging against the building, talking as Pappy and Corcoran walked up. One, a squat gentleman with an eye patch, had two large pistols tucked in his waist band and the other, carrying a shotgun, was tall, rangy, and had anger written all over his face.

"Help you with something?" The man with the eye patch snarled.

"Looking for Maldonado," Corcoran answered. Corcoran thought twice before answering, wondering why someone would even ask.

"Nobody here today." Just as the man said it, Jaime Maldonado stepped out the door and greeted Corcoran and Somerset.

"Why did you say that?" Corcoran growled.

"What's going on?" Maldonado asked, looking at the both men. "Speak up Simpson."

"He just tried to tell me you weren't here, Jaime," Corcoran said. He turned to the man with the patch. "Why, mister. Who are you, and you better start talking."

"His name's Ed Simpson and I believe he's one of those that buys cattle from Mercer, Whitney, and Hatch. The other's name is Slim Nestor, also a buyer." Maldonado was tensed and ready for anything that might happen when Angry Bear came out of the building.

"Hey, One Eye Simpson, you sumbitch man," and he

stepped forward to drive a fist into his good eye. Corcoran grabbed him and held him tight. "No, no, Corcoran, this man sells cattle that is supposed to be our allotment. No, I will kill him now." He struggled but to no avail. Corcoran had a good hold on the strong Indian but had to let go when Slim Nestor brought that shotgun up to shoot the two of them.

Corcoran flung Angry Bear aside and lunged at Nestor, driving the man into the side of the building, knocking the wind from him. Corcoran tore the scattergun from him and slammed it into the side of Nestor's head, knocking him out. Angry Bear took that opportunity to drive his body into Simpson, taking him to the ground.

It took both Maldonado and Pappy Somerset to pull the angry Indian off the so-called cattle buyer. "You got about a minute to get the hell out of here before I turn Angry Bear loose, Simpson. Take that fool Nestor with you." Maldonado wanted to just shoot the man. "We got us one hell of an Indian problem right now and you two are smack in the middle of it. I'll prove that one day soon and when I do, I'll shoot you dead. Now move it," and he pulled his revolver, waving it in the man's face.

Simpson got Nestor to his feet and the two moved off down the street. "I think I should have shot that fool," Corcoran said. "So that's Slim Nestor and One Eye Simpson, eh? Mercer steals cattle and sells them to Hatch for the Indian allotment. Hatch in turn sells most to Nestor and Simpson who sell them on the open market, and everyone makes a dollar or two."

"And we don't eat," Angry Bear snarled. "One man you didn't mention, Corcoran. Lonesome Elk. He a northern Paiute, work for Mercer. We must go now."

"This is one of those few times I hope the army doesn't respond," Pappy murmured. "Whatever is going on is so mucked up now, the army would surely make it worse." He looked at Corcoran with a wry grin. "You suppose these boys have come up with a plan before this big old fight?"

"Sure, by golly, we do," Angry Bear snorted. "You think we not?"

"Not for a minute," Pappy Somerset chuckled. "I'm riding out toward East Gate, Terrence. I'll find Carothers and help get everyone settled there. Are you going with Maldonado to the village?"

"You bet I am. On your way through Dayton let Pa Hennessy know what we're doing and see if he can get enough people together to get that station open and those coaches on the road. That's a mail contract that Major Watson seems to have forgotten about. That was a fool move abandoning that station." He wondered if there was more to it than just riding to help Hog Mercer. Was Watson really as connected to some of Mercer's shady dealings as he was hearing?

He put the thoughts aside to concentrate on the current problems. "It'll take us almost two days to reach the village. Jaime sent wires to Washington and Fort McDermott. Hatch is in Washington and Jaime wants to be on the road before Hatch can wire back telling him to do nothing. We're sure as hell not going to wait for an answer from the army, either."

"We'll ride with you as far as Dayton, Pappy," Jaime said. "Then we're gonna do a little cross-country riding. Angry Bear knows this country far better than any of us."

"Let's ride," Corcoran said getting the group underway.

"We could sit and talk ourselves half to death," he chuckled.

"How many of our young men are missing, Crying Wolf?" Shaking Rocks and several other elders were seated on robes in Crying Wolf's lodge. A fire made the lodge warm despite a cold wind blowing in from the north. "I fear we have created big trouble for the people."

"Three young men returned today and we don't know where ten or twelve others might be. There is no shame in what we did, Shaking Rocks. I would remind all of you of the massacre at the dried lake, of a young girl found dead, and another brutalized by that foul white man, Hog Mercer.

"Do not wait until a situation is over to say you had a better idea. That should have been said at the beginning. We did what needed to be done and it should have ended right then. It was young hot heads eager for that first taste of blood who were wrong. They were rebellious and didn't listen to the thoughts of the elders."

"I meant no criticism of the raid, Crying Wolf," Shaking Rocks said. He took a long draw on a pipe and handed it off. "I do fear the consequences of what the rebellious ones have done. Abducting a white girl when our fight was because of a white man abducting one of our girls could bring the army. We must prepare for that."

"Sending families and small groups into the desert was the right thing to do, Crying Wolf." Dancing Pines was the eldest of the group, from a clan associated with the northern Paiutes. "I have faced the many guns of the army in battle and all of us know there are five, maybe ten times more of them every day. More guns than there are stars in the heavens."

"We cannot fight them and win, Crying Wolf. You must meet with this Maldonado who is coming to the village with a good heart. You have made right an attack on our women by that white man. Our women took him to the fires of hell when you brought him to them. Because of a lack of control over the young and vigorous men of our village, our problem continues."

The rebuke went straight to Crying Wolf's heart and it was quiet in the lodge for several minutes as all let the words linger in their minds. The pipe made a full circle before Crying Wolf said anything.

"I was the leader of the attack on the white men and I stand by what we did. I was the leader of the attacking force and those that went against my wishes are the ones that are wrong. All of us here have seen battle with the white man and in most cases those battles ended badly for us.

"The attack on the Mercer ranch did not end badly. Maybe I was not strong enough to hold the aggressive young men in check. I did my best but each of us can remember that first taste of blood, that first time when all the juices of the body flowed like lava, and only the deaths of our enemy would cool them."

"This is not the time to discuss what was done right or wrong. Shaking Rocks is right in his heart. We must plan now for what might happen because of the Mercer attack. I have sent the people to scatter into the great desert and they will be safe. We will meet with the agency policeman without fear."

The pipe made another round among the elders and

the meeting broke up. Crying Wolf had been chastised but his leadership remained. Shaking Rocks and Dancing Pines had made their thoughts known, and the men left with good hearts. Crying Wolf's thoughts were on tomorrow, not yesterday, as he sat quietly before his fire, chanting softly the prayers of peace with dignity he had learned so many years ago.

Pappy Somerset bought a mule in Dayton and had it packed with enough food for five people for five days when he rode out of Nevada's first organized town. "Ralph and Mrs. Sonnett might just want some of this food." He chuckled then stiffened though when the thought of them not being alive slipped across his mind. "Fightin'," he murmured. "What the hell are we fightin'? Each other. Us humans can be stupid as," and he pondered for just a second before laughing. "Just as stupid as humans."

When the pioneers survived the forty-mile desert and left Rag Town on the Carson River to continue their voyage to California, the next supply stop was Dayton. It was a bustling community that offered anything the California bound emigrant might want or need. It was some of them that ventured into the nearby mountains and discovered the fabulous Comstock Lode.

"Let's get this group moving." Pappy said to Pa Hennessy. He hoped he would find Ralph Carothers and Sarah Sonnett somewhere near that great sand dune on the eastern edge of the Lahontan Valley. "I'll ride with your people as far as Watson's Station, Pa. Looks like your stage company outfitted you pretty well."

"Yep, they did. Line's been down several days now and

they're losing money fast. That mail contract has been jeopardized and the big bosses don't like that. They named me Station Master and I'll guarantee one thing. Watson's Station is gonna be run a little different than it has been."

Pappy had to chuckle at that. Hennessy had two coaches with two teams for each, a remuda of horses to replace those lost, and men and boys to work the stables. "The major wasn't up to running a station in Nevada's outback, Pappy. He thought he was back east somewhere and everything would be done for him. That won't work out here."

Pappy waved back when he continued on the emigrant road and Pa and them turned into the station grounds. "Angry Bear says there might still be some damn fool braves out here looking for scalps, old mule, so we better keep our eyes wide open. You waggle them ears at me if you get a whiff of 'em." Dark thoughts of Carothers alone out on the desert trying to nurse the injured Sarah and Reb Sonnett and knowing there might still be marauding savages about kept him at a steady pace through the broad valley.

The ride across the wide Lahontan Valley was easy on riders and animals and Pappy made camp where the river begins its northerly spread into a great sink. "I won't make East Gate tomorrow," he muttered getting a fire going and a pot of coffee boiling. He had his camp set up so anyone coming in to the fire would be seen some way out. "I'll save the side meat and biscuits for morning," he muttered, throwing some smoked venison in his coffee cup. "This'll do just fine."

The wind picked up during the night and Pappy was awakened more than once because of noises from the wind. It was just as the sky lightened a bit that one particular noise had the old scout out of his blankets, rifle in hand. "That weren't no wind noise," he grumbled.

He slowly inched his way behind some rocks after making his blankets look like he was still in them. There was a stand of stunted cedar behind him, some pines off to the side, and the rocks in front so he felt hidden and he would see anyone approaching. The wind was moaning through the trees and brush, the sky was filled with ragged, storm-etched clouds, and the sun waited for its allotted time to appear.

The wind was playing games with him, he knew, blowing dust and debris into the air, rattling tree branches together, even making the pines sing songs. "Old mama nature having her fun with me this morning," he murmured. His eyes never stopped sweeping the broad expanse of desert.

He was about to blame the noise on the wind again when there was the slightest rustle off to his right, behind the pine trees. He was as tight to those rocks as lichen would be and saw a slight movement of a tree branch. It wasn't the wind this time, he knew, and brought the already cocked rifle up. "Come on, bugger," he murmured, seeing another branch give a slight twitch.

His mule started stomping, let out a long mournful bray that lasted a full thirty seconds, and Pappy saw a form try to untie the noisy critter. One shot through the man's head ended that situation, and that's when Pappy saw a second form moving toward his bedroll fast. His rifle barked knocking the man back ten feet, but not killing him.

The wounded man crab crawled into the brush and

Pappy quickly moved from behind the rocks, around the camp, and into the brush to try to cut off the intruder. He stopped to listen, was as low to the ground as he could get, and heard some moaning just five feet or so in front of him.

Pappy's heart was thumping hard, his breath coming fast, and he forced himself to slow down, to calm those sword edged nerves, and make every move count. He pinpointed the moaning and moved toward it, rifle cocked and ready. Stepping between two large cedar bushes he spotted the Indian, flat on his back, blood pumping from his neck.

"You're just a boy," Pappy said, taking the war club from the wounded warrior. He tried but was unable to stanch the flow of blood and watched the Indian take his last few breaths. "Damn fools," he muttered walking back to get his fire lit and coffee made. "We take their land and then say they're wrong for fighting back. Sure hope Corcoran and Maldonado can put a lid on this one." The coffee was boiling and Pappy was still thinking of the two men he just killed.

"Nothing but boys, little boys," he said, over and over. He couldn't get it out of his head that he just killed two little boys and it bothered him. "I've been tracking these people all my life, been in so many battles and killed so many men," he said to the winds blowing through the desert. "It's the young ones, still so innocent, that bother me. Animals fight one another for the right to mate but humans fight each other over some of the most stupid reasons. Fightin' over being able to spend good times with a pretty girl, hell, that's what it's all about. Fightin' cuz somebody's different than you? Stupid."

He flung his half-cup of now cold coffee into the fire thinking of Angry Bear. "I liked that crotchety old fool. He's one smart Indian and would be a handful in a good fight. If he and I could be friends, there might be help for the human race yet." He was laughing as he got his camp put together.

"I wonder what I'll find at the sand dunes. Old Ralph Carothers was a fighter in his younger days but he's gone soft. He's got Reb and that Johnson feller with him, and Sarah Sonnett gave me the impression she could fight off a tribe or two. If these two boys were at their camp first, I don't want to think about what I might find." He tucked the war club into the pack, planning on keeping it, knowing he would be forced to keep those horrible memories of killing young boys.

The wind blew hard, then harder, the clouds boiled in from the north, and Pappy knew he would be wet and cold by the time he found Carothers. "Summer one day and winter the next," he chuckled as he finished tying off the packs. "Next stop the old Pony Express stop at the dunes, boys. Hope old Ralph's already gone and cozy warm at East Gate."

Corcoran and Angry Bear rode across the wide plains east of Dayton and into the mountains on the north side. Following several long valleys they dropped into the Truckee River canyon late in the evening. "Made better time than I thought," he said, stepping off Rube.

"Yup," is all Angry Bear said. "We be home tomorrow. Sleep now." He was chewing some smoke-dried meat and wrapped himself in a blanket. "Storm and cold tomorrow, Corcoran."

"I can feel it now," Jaime Maldonado said, throwing some wood on the fire. "As many years as I've been around these parts, I'll never get used to the wind. Even the trees grow crooked because of it," he chuckled.

There was a chill to the wind as Corcoran laid out his bedroll. He gnawed on some hard tack, washed it down with cold water, and wished that fire was closer to sit next to. "Storm and cold tomorrow, is the final word, eh? Good night, Angry Bear."

The Indian didn't say a word but Jaime Maldonado had some choice words about the wind and no hot meat for supper. "Ain't civilized," were his final words before pulling a blanket over his head.

Corcoran was up before Angry Bear and had a good fire going. "That wind's got a bite to it for sure," he murmured. Coffee was boiling and he fried up some bacon, letting a hard biscuit soak up the grease. The three were sitting close to the fire as the wind whipped through their little camp. All three could feel the threat of rain and snow coming on cold winds.

"Crying Wolf gonna let us just ride in, Angry Bear?"

"Sure, Corcoran. Elders worried."

"As well they should be. That raid could very well bring the army down on your tribe no matter how right the idea of the raid was. Watson's Station was attacked, I was attacked, and others, none of whom had anything to do with Hog Mercer's abduction of little Runs With the Wind. I saved that little girl and Badger wanted me dead."

"All he saw was that you were white, Corcoran. Many in the tribe feel that way. With good reason. What you tell

Crying Wolf?" In Corcoran's mind, Angry Bear was an astute Indian.

"Let's ride," Corcoran said. He let Angry Bear's words float around some as they made their way down the quiet river. *Many whites hate all Indians because of the actions of a few and many Indians hate all whites for the same reason. We are interesting people us human beings. What am I going to tell Crying Wolf, he asked and right at this moment, I don't have the slightest idea. I could try to fill his head with platitudes or make promises that can't be kept.*

I think what I'll do is not say very much of anything and let Crying Wolf tell me what it is we can do to stop this war from happening. He couldn't get it out of his head that hatred of the other could lead to such ends. Wanting to kill others that you've never seen before was the sticking point for the big man.

The Truckee River takes a wide turn north for its final push to Pyramid Lake and the Paiute village. They were about five miles north of the turn when five mounted Indians rode out from a stand of cottonwood trees. The first thing Corcoran noticed was that they weren't painted and didn't make any threatening gestures.

"Our escorts," Angry Bear commented, waving to the group.

The five rode up and one spoke to Angry Bear. He was not a tall man but was hefty and muscular, wore his hair long and tied back with bright ribbon. "This is Heavy Horse. He says Crying Wolf is expecting us and we should hurry."

Heavy Horse carried battle scars on his strong body. Corcoran thought the man was probably in his late thirties and would offer one heck of a fight if they got into it.

Despite the bitter wind that man was wearing just a breach cloth and was wrapped in a wool army blanket. He never looked at Corcoran or Maldonado.

The ride into the village was quick and the few people left turned out to welcome the group. They rode straight to Crying Wolf's lodge and dismounted. Inside they found Crying Wolf and three elders arranged around a warm fire. The wind had built as the day progressed and rain and snow were expected at any minute. Angry Bear did not come into the wigwam with them.

Corcoran and Maldonado took the empty spaces and a pipe was lit and offered to the four points of the compass. It was then passed around before any words were spoken. It was Dancing Pines who began the conversation. "There have been mistakes and wrongs by the people and by the whites, and because of those mistakes there is a threat of war. I am an old man and therefore can be blunt where a younger man might think twice before talking." He was sitting with a straight back, legs folded comfortably, with a solemn look on his craggy old face.

"Too many people have died, too many people have been hurt. We cannot change what has been done, years ago, yesterday. We can only try to make tomorrow safe." He nodded to Shaking Rocks who got up immediately and opened the flap of the wigwam. Corcoran and Maldonado were shocked when Shaking Rocks helped Sandra Watson into the lodge.

"What's the meaning of this?" Jaime Maldonado was half way to his feet when Dancing Pines put a hand on his shoulder, easing him back down. Sandra was bruised, her head injury still easing blood through the bandages, and her eyes were almost closed and purple from the bashing she took from Walks So Soft.

"This is an outrage, Crying Wolf. How dare you invite us to talk peace while abducting a young girl and beating her half to death? Is this your idea of working out a way of avoiding a war?" Maldonado was still struggling to get up but Dancing Pines was holding him with strong hands.

"This is not what it seems," Dancing Pines said just loud enough to quiet the agency policeman. "Please let us explain, Maldonado." The agency policeman slowly let himself back down on the robes, but never took his angry eyes from Crying Wolf.

"Whoever is responsible for this will be charged, Crying Wolf. I will leave here with prisoners. Explain yourself." Maldonado had no intention of letting his anger cool down and was ready to arrest everyone in that lodge.

"Your anger is justified, Jaime Maldonado," Crying Wolf said quietly. He let Shaking Rocks get the girl situated and comfortable before continuing. She never uttered a word, kept her eyes lowered, and whimpered softly. "You are facing what we have faced and it isn't right. I led the attack on Hog Mercer because of what he did to two of our young women.

"I was unable to control the young braves who rode with us and they attacked a white group and abducted this young girl. They called it retribution, but it is important for you to know that I, and the elders of this tribe, call it criminal. The young brave who brought this girl here as a trophy is no longer with us." He paused to let those words sink in. "The girl's wounds have been doctored, but the wounds that can't be seen will be with her for a long time."

All eyes were on Sandra who was sobbing now, shaking

all over, not looking at anyone. Jaime Maldonado looked at Corcoran, Dancing Pines, Sandra, and finally Crying Wolf. "Who is responsible for this abduction and these terrible wounds?"

"He was called Walks So Soft," Crying Wolf said. "He is no longer. My apology is not for what he did, it is for not being the leader I should have been. There were several young men who broke away after the Mercer raid, and I'm responsible for allowing that."

"You were warned that this would happen, Crying Wolf." Corcoran spoke for the first time. "I was attacked by Badger who sat with us at your fire. Others attacked Watson's Station. Are there still groups of marauding warriors riding through the Lahontan Valley?"

"I was not aware of Badger's attack on you nor the attack on Watson's Station," Crying Wolf said. He looked to Shaking Rocks and Dancing Pines to say something. The situation was far worse than he first thought.

"It is the army that we fear," Dancing Pines said. He was a dignified old man, had been in many fights and wars with white men, with other tribes, and saw the situation deteriorating quickly. "How do we end this?"

"The army will want someone to stand responsible." Corcoran said this as quietly as possible so the meaning would be fully understood. It was the tribe's responsibility to make the white community, in particular the army, aware that a wrong had been committed and a guilty party was in the Indian Agent's custody. Not the concept of a dead Indian, even if that was the truth of the matter, but a real person or persons that could be prosecuted.

The army was sure to insist on nothing less than warm bodies to blame for what had happened and everyone sitting around the fire knew that for a fact. In the very recent past every elder knew that the army had ridden into Paiute camps and killed every living person without benefit of warning, including women and children. The elders, the headman, Corcoran, and Maldonado knew that whoever was offered would die. The army would accept nothing less.

Corcoran saw Crying Wolf stiffen at his words and understood that he alone was responsible for the raid on Mercer's ranch and for allowing the small groups of renegades to run wild through the Lahontan Valley. Men and women died, and worst of all, in the white army's minds, a young white girl was abducted and abused.

"We will talk," Dancing Pines said. The comment included dismissal of Corcoran and Maldonado from the meeting. This was now purely Paiute business and white men were not included. Corcoran and Maldonado were escorted to another wigwam along with Sandra Watson. Runs With the Wind greeted them and they found Angry Bear at the fire as well.

CHAPTER FIFTEEN

Lieutenant Spencer Knightbridge led his patrol out of Fort McDermitt two hours before sunrise for the long ride to Pyramid Lake. His orders were rather simple in their language but bode ill for the Paiute tribe: "End possible uprising. Use whatever force necessary. Indian Affairs contact: Joseph Hatch, agent. Jaime Maldonado, agency police."

Knightbridge was an academy graduate and had seen service in the Black Hills, Nebraska, and Texas before being assigned to this God-forsaken Ft. McDermitt in the wilds of northern Nevada. His family's ten acres in Vermont had more trees and grass than the entire state of Nevada he often said around the officer's mess. He had fifteen mounted men, five Shoshone scouts, and a supply wagon in his command and was told the First Nevada Volunteers from Carson City would join him on the ride to Pyramid Lake.

Both units were under Major General Orville Rand,

Pacific Command. Following the closing of Fort McChurchill, the Nevada Command under Major James McPherson was reduced to Fort McDermitt in northeastern Nevada, and First Nevada Volunteers headquartered in Carson City.

In several battles in Texas and New Mexico, routing the Comanche and Apache raiders, Lieutenant Knightbridge had a reputation of attack first, take no prisoners, and always lead the charge. Battle ribbons decorated his dress uniform and he was anticipating captain's bars soon. Order and discipline were words to live by.

Knightbridge drove straight for the Black Rock Desert and planned to head due south from there the following day. He held a casual meeting at supper with his three sergeants. "Without the slightest provocation, Crying Wolf attacked the Mercer Ranch and burned it to the ground killing everyone there. He also attacked Watson's Station, a stage stop with a mail contract. There've been no word on casualties at Watson's."

"The latest word from the Indian agent is that the Paiutes have been holding a white girl from Watson's Station. We can anticipate a strong defense from the savages. According to that rider late this afternoon, the First Nevada Volunteers will meet us at what's called Winnemucca Lake on the east side of Pyramid Lake. Send our scouts out tonight. I want to know what's going on in that village well before we get there."

"How many men are with the First Nevada Volunteers?" first Sergeant Michael Ramsay asked. Ramsay was a twenty-year man looking to spend the rest of his life in the army. He loved fighting and drinking, gave every young officer he ever served under holy hell as often as he could, and was feared by every man in his unit.

"There was no mention of numbers in the message, Ramsay. You wouldn't be worried, would you, now?"

Ramsay pretended fear amid the laughter that rang out around the fire. "Ah, sir, you did get me on that one, but I'll still protect you from those feisty Indians when we meet up. Should we break into two fronts on the attack?"

"That would be my first thought, but I'll wait until we know how many the Nevada First brings along. I'll have command, so we'll wait. If they have a fair number with them we'll attack in two waves and really I can't go any farther along in planning than that."

The rest of the evening was spent in small talk and the camp was quiet not long after sunset. Guards were posted, fires were kept low, and the Shoshone scouts were sent out at dark.

Knightbridge hadn't been in a good fight since leaving New Mexico Territory and was itching for this one. The lamp burned late that night in his tent as he poured over the maps of the area. "Various sand dunes around the east side of the lake, rocky mountains coming right down to the shoreline in places, and not much room for sweeping moves. "Our best bet will be to either draw them out into that dry lake bed or drive right through the village in two or three waves."

He made light pencil marks on the maps and leaned back in his camp chair. "I like the second idea best. Kill every person in the village instead of just drawing out the so-called warriors. They'll learn what the army's version of warrior is when I'm through with 'em," he chuckled, blowing out the lamp.

. . .

Angry Bear had tears across his broad cheeks as he tied Crying Wolf's hands behind his back and helped the former headman onto his horse. Maldonado took the lead rope from him and started the long journey to Carson City where the Paiute leader would stand trial for the raids on ranches and the deaths of white men and women.

"You make the best time possible, Jaime. I'll take Sandra Watson back to the station. Ma Hennessy will be able to take care of her. I'll meet you in Carson City just as soon as I can. We have to keep the army from responding to this outbreak."

"I agree, Corcoran. I hope Hatch has responded to my messages. He should be doing all this."

"I'm glad he's not," Corcoran chuckled getting a wry smile from Maldonado.

At a conference the night before, Shaking Rocks and Dancing Pines made it clear that no one would interfere with Maldonado's ride to the capitol. "Angry Bear will ride with you. I can send five more braves as escort if you wish," Dancing Pines said. "No harm will come to you or Crying Wolf."

"I appreciate your cooperation in this horrible situation, Dancing Pines, and I value your word. Angry Bear will be a fine escort and I don't anticipate any problems in Carson City." He had to chuckle to himself thinking how different that ride might be if Pappy Somerset was along to continue his debates on the human animal with Angry Bear.

The ride was as Maldonado said, without problems and

Crying Wolf was behind bars to await trial the next day. Maldonado was informed that the army was planning to take action against the Paiute tribe and the First Nevada Volunteers were going to be involved.

There was no communication from Joseph Hatch, supposedly still in Washington living the good life. Maldonado was on his own as he had been since this business started. He saw to it that the proper wires were sent, paperwork was up to date, and in his words, "my behind is protected, to a degree."

He hurried to the headquarters of the First Nevada Volunteers for an interview with Major James McPherson. McPherson was regular army, spent time in the Dakota Territory as well as Oregon, Idaho, and Wyoming. He had no hatred of Indians but would fight as hard as any man when ordered to do so.

"You have Crying Wolf in custody? That certainly changes the picture, eh?" McPherson invited Captain Oly Hochstettler into the office and introduced the agency policeman. "How many men in your detachment, Captain?"

"I was planning on taking fifty men and some support people, Major. The Paiutes haven't been giving any trouble lately. I'm not sure this is a true uprising."

"It isn't," Maldonado said. "The raid on the Mercer ranch was in retaliation for Mercer abducting another Indian girl and abusing her. It got out of hand, Crying Wolf lost control of his young warriors, and two other small attacks were made. Unfortunately there were deaths and of course property damage.

"The Paiute elders insisted that Crying Wolf be held

responsible and I have him in custody at this time. Unfortunately, again, the commander at Fort McDermitt is not aware of that."

Hochstettler stiffened at the news. "My God, Major. I was told that Lieutenant Knightbridge is already on the march and I was leaving within the hour to join him for a punishment attack."

"Move your command, Captain, put it under command of the highest ranking officer, and you and Maldonado ride like the wind to intercept Knightbridge." McPherson sat down and took pen in hand, writing furiously for several minutes. "These are your orders, they countermand anything Knightbridge might have from McDermitt. Go now."

"I'll meet you at the agency building in ten minutes, Jaime," Hochstettler said. "Pack as light as you can."

Maldonado rode into the agency yards to find Terrence Corcoran stepping down from a foam-flecked Rube. "About time you got here. You two better get fresh horses, we've got a hard ride ahead, Terrence. I'll explain on the way. Angry Bear, saddle up, you'll need to guide us back to the village by the absolute fastest route."

Corcoran ran to the agency stables, found a good-looking bay gelding and got him saddled up. Angry Bear was right with him and the two were mounted and ready to ride when Captain Hochstettler rode in. Maldonado ran from the building and jumped on his horse.

"Let's go, Jaime. Who's this?" Hochstettler was unsettled seeing another civilian and an Indian ready to ride.

Maldonado made the introductions and filled Corcoran and Angry Bear in on what was going on as they left Carson City at a fast trot. "I've heard about you, Corcoran. You have an interesting reputation. You shot the sheriff you worked for?"

"Long story, Captain," Corcoran chuckled, "but I surely did do that. What's happened these last few days is a serious incident but not an Indian uprising and retribution is not called for."

"I agree and so does Major McPherson. The problem we have right now is finding Knightbridge before that hothead attacks the village. He's got a small detachment with enough fire power to go in without waiting for us, and he's got enough blood in his eyes to do that."

Angry Bear led them across the range of mountains separating the Carson River from the Truckee River canyon pushing their horses to their limits. Night was falling and the trail became hard to see. It was Hochstettler who called a halt to the ride. "We're gonna kill these horses or one of us if we keep this up. Let's rest for a short time, have some coffee, and then continue."

"Nothing will happen before late tomorrow at the earliest. Knightbridge should be in the Black Rock Desert tonight. We were scheduled to meet at the Winnemucca Lake late tomorrow."

"I think it would be a good idea to let Angry Bear ride on in to the village and alert the elders that we are coming and to be aware of Knightbridge's detachment. We'll be just a couple of hours behind him. Shaking Rocks and Dancing Pines can keep the village peaceful." Corcoran held those two in high regard after the way they handled the Crying Wolf affair.

"Good." Maldonado said. "Tell them everything, Angry

Bear. Make sure they understand the danger and that we are coming to try and end this threat."

A fire was lit and coffee was boiling in minutes. The horses were picketed in grass along the bank of the Truckee River and the men softened some jerky in their hot coffee and were asleep in minutes.

CHAPTER SIXTEEN

Lieutenant Knightbridge had his company up and ready for the ride as the sun made its way across a vast Nevada sky. The patrol was near the black rock that gave the desert its name and had a long ride ahead of them to make Winnemucca Lake, what the Indians called the desert lake, in time to meet up with the First Nevada Volunteers. "What's the word from the scouts?"

"Too early, Lieutenant. We won't hear from them before this afternoon. The supply wagon has a bad wheel and will be left here. We'll split up the supplies and turn the horses into pack animals. They'll end up several hours behind us since the teamsters will have to walk the animals." Sergeant Ramsay almost had a smirk on his face saying it, but the darkness kept Knightbridge from seeing it.

"Get the men fed and we'll mount up in twenty minutes. I want that village leveled tonight and everyone in it dead. Stragglers will be whipped and court-martialed."

"Yes sir," Ramsay said. *Man's bucking hard for those*

captain's bars. More than one of these men in this command would be willing to put a piece of lead in his back. This is gonna be another blood-bath I'm afraid. Ramsay had seen more combat than any officer within five hundred miles and knew the Paiutes were good fighters. He also knew they could not stand up to the massive firepower of the army.

It was a forced march with few rest stops as the patrol made its way across the flat and barren Black Rock Desert and late afternoon before they left the desert floor. They had to make their way through brush and rocks, over low-lying hills, slowly working their way toward the desert lake. They were intercepted by three of the Shoshone scouts as the day slowly tried to end.

"You saw three white men ride into the Paiute village?" Knightbridge wasn't sure he understood the scout. "Then what?"

"Taken to meeting of elders. They come this way now. We ride hard to get here first."

Knightbridge was in his command squad tent when the scout was brought in. "Well, get something to eat and stay close." He hollered out for Sergeant Ramsay who was standing outside the tent. "We may have visitors coming. The scouts say three white men came into the village, met with the chief, and are now coming our way. Probably some damn do-gooders, but treat them well."

"Bring them to you?"

"Hell, no, Ramsay. Just listen to what they have to say, give 'em some water, and send 'em on their way. We're moving before sunrise tomorrow. We'll find the First and prepare our attack."

Sergeant Ramsay had two men join him and walked

toward where riders might come from. "Three white people coming. Don't shoot 'em."

"There's dust about half a mile out, Sergeant. Whoever it is, they're coming hard, it looks like."

Hochstettler, Corcoran, and Maldonado rode in at a solid lope, all three jumping from their horses when Ramsay held them up. "Jesus," Ramsay snarled and snapped to attention when he saw captains bars on Hochstettler's uniform.

"Take us to Lieutenant Knightbridge immediately, Sergeant."

"Take care of their horses, Private. Follow me sir," Ramsay said, leading them through the bustling camp. Knightbridge's orderly snapped to attention and opened the tent flap.

"What's this?" Knightbridge was about to chew some butt when Hochstettler stepped into the squad tent. "Oh, sorry, sir," he said, standing up.

"I'm Captain Hochstettler, First Nevada Volunteers, Lieutenant. Let's sit around your fire out front. We have much to discuss. Have your orderly bring chairs and invite your first sergeant to join us, please."

Knightbridge frowned at the intrusion but recognized authority and had his men make a comfortable setting around the fire for these visitors. When everyone was settled and the fire was blazing, Hochstettler pulled the papers from Major McPherson from his blouse. "These orders are from Major James McPherson," he said, handing the papers to Knightbridge. "I'm now in command, Lieutenant and ordering this unit to stand down.

"There is to be no attack on the Paiute village. The rest of my command should be riding into the village about now. The leader of the limited uprising is in custody, and most of those who took part are either dead or are in custody as well."

"My orders are from Captain Henry Caldwell, Fort McDermitt. I don't accept orders from the First Nevada Volunteers," Knightbridge said. His eyes were narrowed and his thin lips were curled in a sneer that could fry an egg.

Corcoran and Maldonado stiffened at the comment and the look on the young Lieutenant's face. There was the slightest smile on Corcoran's mug and he wondered whether Hochstettler would shoot the man or follow army protocol.

"I command the First Nevada Volunteers, Lieutenant. Major McPherson commands the Nevada Division, Pacific Command. Your Captain Caldwell works for McPherson. Do I make myself clear?"

"I'm Jaime Maldonado representing the Nevada Indian Agent, sir. Those responsible for the problems are in custody or are dead. It will be up to a court to determine any further punishment. The Indian Affairs Agent will see to it that any and all involved will face legal justice."

Knightbridge sat rigid in his canvas camp chair, glaring first at Hochstettler then Maldonado. Sergeant Ramsay sat quietly listening carefully. More than once he has seen officers get in a twit and lose everything. Would Knightbridge? It wouldn't surprise him, not in the least. The man had a blood lust, seemed to thrive on killing, particularly killing Indians. He caught the wry look on Corcoran's face and had a hard time hiding a slight grin.

Corporal Leon Smith walked up to the gathering. "Sir, the men are assembled and ready for retreat. Your orders?"

Smith was near thirty, a redhead with a barrel chest and jutting jaw. He was from the Boston waterfront, and spent time along the Texas-Mexico border fighting anyone and everyone.

"Tell the men to stand down, Corporal," Captain Hochstettler said before Knightbridge could answer. He turned to Knightbridge. "Send a small detachment to Fort McDermitt detailing what has happened, Lieutenant. Include a copy of Major McPherson's orders.

"First Sergeant," he said turning to Ramsay. Ramsay jumped to attention. "See to it the men understand there have been a change of command and a change of orders. Prepare the camp to remain here until we hear from either Captain Caldwell or Major McPherson. And, Smith, sound retreat."

"Yes, sir," Ramsay said. He saluted, never looked at Knightbridge, and trotted off with Corporal smith.

"Lieutenant, let's you and I take a little walk, eh?" Hochstettler planned to explain the facts of life to the man without others hearing his tirade. "I too am a graduate of the Academy, a regular army officer, and at this time next week, sir, will be a major. My boss, McPherson will be jumped to colonel, and unless your attitude changes quickly, you will be a lieutenant for many, many years.

"Do I make myself clear?"

"We will stay here until we hear from Caldwell and McDermitt. Are you planning to simply let those Indians get away with kidnapping and abusing a white girl? Burning out a white rancher? Attacking a stagecoach station? I would not believe an officer of the United States army would do such a cowardly thing."

Hochstettler stopped instantly, turned, and drew his

sabre, glaring at the feisty lieutenant. Knightbridge stepped back and started for his and Captain Hochstettler slowly put his back.

"Stand at attention, Lieutenant. We're alone, so no one has seen or heard what just went on. Another statement like that and you'll be in irons, Lieutenant. I'll see to it that you will never dis-honor another uniform nor receive another salute." Anger boiled through Hochstettler and he was fighting harder than he had ever fought to keep from killing this impudent fool on the spot.

"There are actions in this situation that you are unaware of, things that have been done that you don't know about. If you ever suggest that I or Major McPherson are cowards again, I'll have those bars ripped from you and you'll be drummed out."

Hochstettler allowed himself to cool out some as he and Knightbridge walked slowly around the camp's perimeter. He spent that half hour explaining what had been taking place over the past few days. Knightbridge walked stiffly alongside his superior officer, listening but not accepting most of what he heard.

"You're an arrogant and impudent man, Lieutenant, unwilling to accept changes." Captain Hochstettler's many years were going to be tested by this willful young officer. "I will expect nothing but cooperation and respect as we bring this situation to a conclusion."

They made their way through the camp and toward Knightbridge's tent and command compound. "Sir," Sergeant Ramsay said, "I've assigned Corporal Smith and Private Owens to carry your dispatch to Fort McDermitt. Will there be anything else?"

"No," Hochstettler said. "In the morning I want to address the men. I'm sure there's been a lot of speculation in the last couple of hours," he chuckled. "We'll do a full inspection and I'll explain why the changes." Ramsay hightailed it out of officer country before anything else happened.

"Lieutenant Knightbridge, I will accept nothing but full support from you. Good evening," Hochstettler said and walked toward the tent that had been set up for he and the others.

"You gonna shoot him?" Corcoran chuckled when the captain walked in. "Man's got himself one hell of an attitude. He came for a war, Captain, just like the young warriors who rode with Crying Wolf."

"He's a bit testy," Hochstettler laughed. "He's a professional soldier, though. I'm sure he'll change his attitude when he sleeps on what I said. What are your plans, Corcoran? Not much reason to hang around here. I need Jaime Maldonado to be with us."

"We left people scattered from the Carson River to Carroll Summit, Captain, and some of them are injured and vulnerable. We don't know if all the raiders are accounted for, and I got to get away from that Knightbridge before I hurt him." He chuckled some but knew he was telling the truth.

"I'll grab an early breakfast, pack some trail food, and be gone. I've got my own horse in Carson City, my own pack mule at Watson's Station, and an injured lady that I need to know better somewhere in the great open desert of Nevada. I'm tired just thinking about what I've got to do."

"Who besides the Sonnett woman was injured?"

Hochstettler knew about her injuries and those of Sandra Watson but wasn't aware of others.

"I think Reb Sonnett took a bullet and Abe Johnson got hit as well," Maldonado said.

When you meet up with Lieutenant Ferguson and the First, bring him up to date and have him bring the troops here. We'll give these McDermitt boys a little show."

CHAPTER SEVENTEEN

Joseph Hatch was livid when he was escorted into Major McPherson's office. He arrived in Carson City the night before totally unaware of the attacks and responses. "Just who does Maldonado think he is? Acting as if he were the Indian Agent, not I. And you, Major McPherson, what gives you the authority to send troops to Pyramid Lake?"

"Calm down, Hatch, you're in no position to question what's happened in your absence. You ignored all our efforts to reach you and the situation demanded immediate action." He offered the fat little man a cigar and suggested he sit down and listen. "My orders are from General Rand, Pacific Command. What happened has been brewing for some time, I'm sure you're aware of that. Why didn't you respond to our wires?"

"I don't remember getting any wires, Major."

"Hmmm. Well," McPherson said, holding up a sheaf of papers, "this is a log from the telegraph office indicating every message sent to you in the last seven days and not one response back. General Rand is meeting with your superiors in San Francisco tomorrow, Hatch.

"There have been complaints made that the Paiute tribe has been shorted on its cattle allotments for the last three years. Those complaints have reached Pacific Command and need to be answered. In your absence, Hog Mercer has been killed and the Whitney family also."

"Why are you telling me this?" Hatch was still standing, but his knees went weak hearing of Mercer's death. "Mercer is a cattle rancher. What has that to do with the Bureau of Indian Affairs?" He slumped into the offered chair knowing he should have responded to those many wires he had received while in Washington.

"It has to do with you buying stolen cattle from Mercer. You used government money to buy the cattle that should have gone then to the tribe. Instead, you sold the cattle rather than allotting them to the Indians, sir.'

Hatch jumped to his feet almost biting off the end of his cigar. "You have no proof of any such thing, Major. How dare you accuse me of theft and of selling government property. There is no proof of any such action."

Major McPherson snickered as he walked around his desk. He knew he had his man, but also knew he didn't have the proof he needed. At least not yet. "You'll be receiving wires from General Dodge and your superiors Mr. Hatch. I advise you not to leave Carson City without my approval. You're dismissed."

Hatch was furious, turned, and stormed from the offices of the First Nevada Volunteers to the Lucky Silver Saloon. "I've got to find Slim Nestor at once," he stammered rushing down the street, around the capitol grounds, and into the saloon. "How the hell did

McPherson know about the cattle and Mercer? Damn," he muttered, looking around the smoky barroom. "I'll bet that Maldonado has something to do with this. He's always sticking his nose where it doesn't belong."

Nestor was at a table with One Eye Simpson, sharing a bottle of whiskey. "So, back in town, are we? And just in time, I might add. Heard what's been going on?" Nestor's scowl told Hatch to be very careful with his answers. Slim Nestor had the reputation of a knife man, a gunman, and bragged often about killings in his past. Scars on his face, arms, and body proved to many his often told stories of knife fights.

No one knew exactly where the swarthy man came from or his heritage. His relatives may have come from many of the seven continents, from many colors and races. His enemies swear he is the son of the devil himself.

"I think it would be best if you brought me up to date, Slim. I just left Major McPherson's office and he alluded to some things that could be bothersome."

"Bothersome is it?" Nestor thundered the question. A few heads turned their way at the loud voices. Nestor tried to calm himself. "Sit your butt down, Hatch and listen carefully. I don't intend to go to jail because of you being stupid or arrogant. I'll cut out your heart and eat it before I go to jail because of you. Sit," he commanded again. As the trained dog he was, Hatch sat.

If Hatch was fearful leaving McPherson's office, he was terrified as he sat down next to Slim Nestor. Simpson had the slightest grin on his face watching the chubby little man sink into his chair. Simpson didn't tolerate haughty men who rode high horses. He enjoyed watching them fall hard. Hatch reached for an empty glass and poured some of that golden joy juice in, almost gulping a large dose.

"Tell me what's happened," he coughed out.

Slim watched him pour more whiskey and took his time lighting a cigar. "Most of our organization is dead, Hatch, that's what's happened. Hog Mercer kidnapped another Indian girl but didn't quite get around to killing her. The little darling was found by some damn fool deputy sheriff from Eureka County, and the whole damn tribe descended on Mercer's ranch." He told the story slow, letting the facts come out as from thick fog.

"That's only part of what's happened, Hatch. Want to hear more, do you?" The killer's eyes narrowed down some, as he leaned into Hatch's face, his foul breath almost choking the smug government man. "Our fine Major Watson rode to Hog's defense and got his nasty little ass killed too. Oh, before I forget, Josh Whitney and his wonderful sons are rotting in hell as well."

For the first time in years there was no sneer on Hatch's face, no smug little chin tilts, no shaking of his head. Nestor turned to One Eye Simpson, and with a cruel smirk asked, "Did I forget anything, big Ed?"

"You might have glossed over the investigation of allotment shortages, Slim. That might interest Mr. Hatch some." Simpson was almost chuckling as he said that. "None of this had to happen if you had let Nestor kill Hog Mercer when he killed that first Indian girl. You were warned, Hatch."

"I've got to get to the office," Hatch said. He had to get rid of papers there, had to be alone to think, to make these problems disappear. Account books were filled with pages of sales and distribution records dating back three years that had to be burned, letters and documents between he and Mercer, Watson, and Whitney that had to be gotten rid of. That's one of the problems of being arrogant. He kept all the records so he could gloat over their successes while enjoying some fine brandy in the evenings.

"Slim, you and Simpson come by the office this evening and we'll plan out how to keep ourselves safe. There may be people from San Francisco arriving in the next few days and we have to be prepared for them."

"You run out on us you fat little pig and I'll hunt you down," Nestor growled. "We'll be there at six."

Corcoran picked up his pack mule at Watson's Station and rode into Carson City, headed for the Indian Agency compound to find Rube. "It'll be a fine ride out to East Gate," he said, looking forward to the ride and meeting up with Sarah Sonnett. It was a slow ride down busy Carson Street, and he stopped when he was hailed by a voice he didn't recognize.

"You the deputy from Eureka County?" Ormsby County Sheriff Sydney Cochran said, dodging through traffic to stand near Corcoran's horse. Ormsby County wasn't a large piece of real estate but it was home to the state capitol, had a shoreline tax value at Lake Tahoe, and had rail access to the intercontinental railroad. In Cochran's mind it was a very important piece of real estate.

Corcoran eyed the heavy-set sheriff and knew he would be in one good long fight if he tangled with him. "Yup, that would be me," he smiled. "Name's Corcoran, Terrence Corcoran. What can I do for you, Sheriff?" He pulled his horse and trailing mule out of the traffic and toward a hitch rail and stepped off.

"Well, for one thing, you can stop meddling in business that isn't any of your concern," Cochran said.

"And just what business would that be?"

"You're meddling in Indian affairs, Corcoran. I've heard about you. I've heard all the stories and I don't want the kind of trouble you bring. You stay out of Ormsby County business."

"Indian affairs are not Ormsby County business and my affairs are none of your business, Sheriff. I have business with Major McPherson and with the Indian Affairs officer, not you."

"I'll be keeping my eyes on you, Corcoran." Sydney Cochran stood about five feet and ten inches but weighed in at a solid two hundred pounds. He was a woodcutter in the Tahoe Basin forests before giving it up for the badge. Many a man went to jail with lumps and bruises from a tumble with Cochran.

"You do that, Sheriff, you know, just in case someone sneaks up behind me." He stepped back on his horse and rode to the Indian Agency compound. He wondered how it was the sheriff even knew that he was about. He found Rube in a stall and was giving the gelding a good rub down before saddling up. "Three day's of oats and you'll be a handful, eh? We'll work 'em out of you."

"Say, there. Who are you and what are you doing?"

Corcoran turned to find a fat little man in a rumpled suit standing at the barn doors. His linen white face carried a scowl that wouldn't frighten anything and Corcoran almost laughed right out. "Just pickin' up my horse. Who might you be?" He untied Rube and walked toward the big doors.

Hatch spotted the badge immediately. "You're on federal property, mister, and I'm asking the questions."

"I'm glad you are, but since you won't tell me who you are, go straight to hell and get out of my way"

"I happen to be Joseph P. Hatch, Indian Agent for Nevada, and you're on federal property without permission. I'll hold you for the sheriff."

"So you're the one responsible for all this mess, eh?" Corcoran tied Rube off and turned back to Hatch. "You and I have a lot to talk about, sir. Let's go into your office and discuss this mess you've caused." Corcoran turned the man by his shoulders and pushed him toward the office steps. We've got some angry people runnin' around out in that wide open country called Nevada. Some want your hide, just as I do."

They made their way into Hatch's office and Corcoran pushed the man into his chair. It was only about fifteen minutes later that Corcoran left the office and mounted Rube.

CHAPTER EIGHTEEN

"I say we just kill the fat little bastard and ride off, Slim. There ain't nothing holding us here now that Mercer, Watson, and Whitney are dead. He's in his office burning all the evidence, let's let him finish that," and he snickered, just thinking about it, "and put a knife or two through his black little heart."

Slim Nestor was chuckling softly as he refilled his glass. He and One Eye clinked their glasses and took long slow drinks of hot whiskey. "Yeah, Big Ed," Slim laughed, "I think that would be best. He should have a considerable amount of cash in that office as well." Their lucrative operation was over, they knew that, and they knew Hatch would tell the world all about it with one good slap across his fat jowls. Or a well placed knee somewhere else.

"There are at least fifty head of cattle down at the stockyards, Ed. Guess we'll just have to leave 'em there. Damn." He sat back thinking, took at couple more sips of whiskey and smiled an ugly snarl at One Eye Simpson. "We'll kill that fat little snipe, ride to Reno and catch a train to Denver, and see what that fine city has to offer, eh?"

"We want to make sure he has time to burn all those papers first, though," Simpson said. He sat back and smiled at the thought of a long train ride through the Rocky Mountains. "It's been a good fight, though. Three years making good money while Mercer and them did all the work."

"I would just as soon not hear that name again," Nestor said. "We both knew he should have been killed after that first incident with the little Indian girl." His anger settled a bit with a large dose of whiskey. "They got some really big stockyards in Denver, from what I've heard. Shouldn't be too hard workin' something out."

"For the record, Mr. Hatch, I'm Terrence Corcoran a deputy sheriff out of Eureka County and for the last several days I've been involved in a swamp of filth brought about by you. Your agency lawman, Jaime Maldonado and I have fought with, cajoled, and broken bread with Paiute leaders and warriors. We've buried dead cattle rustlers and saved young girls."

Corcoran took a long breath, shoved Joe Hatch into a chair and took one himself. He sat back with a smile and leaned forward toward the agent. "You on the other hand have been back east living the good life, drinking fine wine, smoking Virginia tobacco, and dancing with fair maidens. The party's over, Hatch. I know about the stolen cattle scheme, know about the allotment shortages, even know about the two so-called buyers you work with."

"Prove it," is all Hatch said. All the arrogance and self-assuredness returned, and he reached for a cigar, the slightest smile across his fat face. "Talk is cheap, deputy."

The big right fist came out of nowhere slamming into the side of Hatch's head. The cigar went flying across the room and Hatch was right behind it, flopping around on the wooden floor. He was unconscious and would be for some time, Corcoran figured. He started going through the desk drawers and then a file cabinet behind the desk.

"Oh, my," he whispered, opening a file folder marked Cattle Payments. "That fool kept records of the rustling operations, the selling and reselling of the cattle, even how the shortages to the Indians were covered up. Major McPherson wanted proof, did he? Well, wait until he sees this."

He made sure the inert Mr. Hatch was still breathing and walked out the door and across to the First Nevada Volunteers headquarters. "That fool must be about as arrogant as I've run into in a long time. He even has names, dates, and amounts listed in these accounts." Corcoran was walking fast but paging through the various papers inside the files. "He's the type that would tell you about every single penny he pilfered," he chuckled.

"My God, Corcoran," McPherson said, paging through the file. "What have you done with Hatch?"

"I left him right where he fell. I'm not sure where we go from here, Major. I can't arrest the man anymore than you can. I might be a deputy sheriff, just not in this county. Do we call Cochran?"

McPherson called his orderly in and had him send for the sheriff. "Don't take any guff from that old badger.

Bring him here, pronto." He sat back in his chair chewing on a cigar, smiling. "I've waited a long time for what's in these papers, Corcoran. They had a good operation, one that was difficult to see because there was so much going on. Cattle being rustled is one thing, a major crime, but then selling the cattle to the government without any questions asked compounds the issue."

"I'm sure that when Mercer ran people off their ranches and simply took over their herds, he kept using their brands. On paper, Major, there were no stolen cattle. He didn't have to make runnin' iron or nothing. From just glancing at those papers I'd say Hatch paid top dollar, government money, for whatever Mercer and Whitney brought him." Corcoran was shaking his head not willing to accept that no one ever questioned any of Hatch's deals.

"Then withholding most of the Indian cattle allotment and reselling it on the open market through that bastard Slim Nestor was the icing on that putrid cake."

The major was shaking his head right along with Corcoran. Will you join me in a little splash of some brandy?" He reached into the bottom drawer of his desk and brought out a fine crystal decanter about half full. Two cups materialized in moments and they toasted their good luck.

They were on their second toast when Sydney Cochran was ushered into the office. "What's this all about, McPherson? Oh, and you, Corcoran, too. This better be worth my time."

McPherson never did much care for the Ormsby County sheriff and took great pleasure in simply handing him the file. He and Corcoran sipped their brandy while the sheriff read then re-read the pages that detailed three years of corruption in his jurisdiction. He slipped the papers back in the file and stood up looking back and forth at the two men.

"Well, are you coming with me to arrest Mr. Hatch or just sit there with your brandy."

On the short walk to the agency compound Corcoran detailed what had been going on over the last few days and McPherson backed him up with some comments of his own. "In fact, Sheriff, you have Crying Wolf in your jail right now on a federal hold." Corcoran appreciated the way the sheriff's attitude had changed. From a bully to a working lawdog, he thought and smiled just a bit. "Jaime Maldonado should be back in town tomorrow or the next day if everything goes right with the army."

"I wonder if Hatch has been holding back on cattle allotments to all the tribes in Nevada?" the sheriff muttered. "The Western Shoshone and Washoe are large tribes like the Paiute." They were about fifty feet or so from the agency offices and watched two men saunter in.

"That feller with eye patch is One Eye Simpson and the other is a very dangerous killer named Slim Nestor," Corcoran said. "They are full partners with Hatch. I think we better hurry along, gents."

There was obvious scuffling going on in the office as they approached and Corcoran pulled his big Colt and ran for the doors with Cochran at his heels. The Major was just steps behind as they burst in. Nestor dropped the bloody knife and pulled his pistol, shooting Syd Cochran in his gun arm,

Simpson pulled his weapon and died with one shot from Corcoran, but Nestor dove through a window, breaking the glass and tumbling into the rocks below. He was on his feet and into the agency barn, found a horse all saddled and rode him out the back doors.

Corcoran went through the same window hollering at McPherson to round up some help. Rube was tied up at McPherson's rack a block away and Corcoran raced for him, and was on Nestor's trail. "The man went north when he rode out of the barn," he muttered, kicking Rube into a full out run. "Will he go straight or will he turn east toward Dayton?"

Corcoran was stretched out across Rube's neck urging that hard riding gelding into an even faster run. "Hurry, boy, we got to get close enough to see which way that fool runs. Hurry, now." It was people on the side of the road that told Corcoran which way, with them all looking in the same direction, even pointing.

The road north would lead through Washoe Valley and around the big lake, and toward Reno. "Mistake number one, Slim Nestor," Corcoran said right out loud. It was a long thirty miles from Carson City to Reno and unlike the eastern road, this one would be filled with people, horses, wagons, even railroad trains.

"I hope McPherson is smart enough to send out some wires while he gathers a posse. We're riding into a rather populated area of this big old state, pardner," he muttered.

As Corcoran neared Lakeview Hill he spotted Nestor about half a mile ahead of him riding at a comfortable lope. "So, old man, you're not willing to kill your horse, eh? Good for you." He let Rube come down to a lope as well, planning on closing the gap between them without letting Nestor know he was on his tail.

. . .

"Is he dead?" Cochran was trying to put a rag on his arm wound while McPherson was checking on Joseph Hatch.

"No, but he sure as hell should be. That knife went deep but he's breathing. One of us has got to get some help, Sheriff. He's gonna bleed to death without a doctor, and Corcoran is gonna need help, too."

Cochran checked to make sure Simpson was dead and walked toward the door. "I'll get a doctor and get a posse up, too, Major. You stay here with Hatch and do what you can." The sheriff found he didn't have enough strength to run and walked toward his office near the capitol building as fast as he could. The bleeding continued and he was stumbling when he broke through the door.

"Need help," he moaned and fell to the floor. Two deputies jumped from their desks and ran to him. "Get a doctor to the Indian Agent's office quickly," he said to the first one there, Jim Dorsey. "Sandy," he said to the other. "Listen carefully." He was having a hard time fighting to stay conscious. "Hatch knifed. Slim Nestor running. Corcoran trying to catch. Notify Washoe City and Reno. Go, man."

"Corcoran? Terrence Corcoran? What's he doing here?" Sandy White remembered Corcoran from his days in Virginia City.

"Just get help and follow. Corcoran will need help. Started north. Send someone for doctor for me."

White ran to the back of the jail and found a jailer, told him what happened and sent him for a doctor. He found his horse and rode down to the telegraph office and notified authorities to the north, then hit the Silver Saddle Saloon and gathered a few men for a posse. "Meet me at the Indian Agency barn in ten minutes. We'll be riding hard boys."

Sandy White was almost forty years old, chief deputy in the capital for several years, and had an interest in one mine on the Comstock and one ranch in the Carson Valley. His plan was to retire on that ranch before the end of the coming summer. He came into this law business after working in the mines and was as tough as the rock he used to break.

"Alright, men, listen up. Slim Nestor knifed the Indian Agent, stole a horse from this barn, and rode out. He's being followed by a deputy sheriff out of Eureka County. What we don't know is whether Nestor rode north or east. Let's ride to the intersection and maybe someone can tell us. If not, I'll split the posse to cover both roads."

He led seven men north toward the intersection and it took less than a minute to discover which way Nestor and Corcoran headed. There were still people talking about the two riders coming hell bent for election right through town. "It's a long ride, men, so let's not kill the horses. A solid trot will eat up those miles and Nestor won't run his horse into the ground either."

"Why would he run toward Reno?" Fred Dawson asked.

"Maybe thinks he can hide in the crowds," Sandy White laughed. "I alerted the Washoe County Sheriff that he's coming their way. We'll get him."

There was a tremendous amount of activity in Washoe Valley. Flumes brought hundreds of logs down from the Carson Range of the Sierra Nevada to be floated to nearby mills. The milled timbers were then freighted to Virginia City where they fed great steam engines and were used to hold up the mines. The Sierra Nevada around Lake Tahoe was stripped bare of timber.

Ranches along the western edge of the valley were home to large herds of cattle and the grass was thick. Spring was working its way into being which meant that thousands of calves were also running through the valley. "He has to be making for Reno," Sandy White said.

"Think he knows he's being followed?" somebody asked.

"He has to. You heard Major McPherson say he dove through that window and raced for the barn. Nestor is more than just a dangerous man, he's a sneaky, back-stabbing killer, so when we find him, he'll be fighting back like a trapped badger."

Nestor's stolen horse was breathing hard, not quite heaving, but would be soon if he kept up the strong pace he was on. He slowed the horse to a walk, letting it catch its breath. He turned in the saddle often, searching behind him for anyone who looked like he was trying to catch up to him. "Where the hell did those men come from? How did they know we were after Hatch?" he asked over and over.

"Ten more minutes and we would have been out of there, Hatch would have been dead, and we'd be making this ride nice and slow. All this because Hog Mercer couldn't keep his pants on." Nestor tried to get his mind off what had happened and onto what he needed to do. "Ain't no way out of this valley that would take me anywhere except north to Reno. I need to hole up somewhere and quickly. Sure as hell there's already a posse somewhere behind me."

The west side of the valley was sprinkled with ranches but there weren't any roads that led up into the steep mountains and he didn't know any of the ranchers. "If I knew any of these people I could just ride in and take over but sure as hell I'd ride into a place with twenty cowboys looking to shoot me."

The main road through the valley was heavily used and in good shape but offered no places to hide out. He was nearing the monster building that miner from Gold Hill built. "Sandy Bowers and his fortune telling woman wasted a lot of money there," he muttered. He thought about riding up into the mountains but wasn't prepared for living that way.

"I've got to find a little place to get into." He was coming up on the Winter's Ranch and Washoe City and saw a little cabin tucked up in the rocks, hundreds of yards off the main road. "Won't be no cowboys with guns there," he snickered, and turned toward the place. The single track up to the cabin was overgrown and Nestor couldn't see any activity around the stone cabin.

His approach was slow and quiet, and he dismounted near a shed that probably doubled as a barn, hay shed, and tool room, and tied the worn out horse to a post. The corral was empty, there wasn't any stored hay or feed sacks around, and no one had started an early spring garden.

"This might be the best part of today," he snickered, slowly advancing on what would be the back door of the small cabin. He peered through a filthy window into a darkened kitchen, could see through and into the front of the building and was sure there was no one home. The door opened easily and he stepped in.

"Nice and quiet, now, mister. Put your hands way up and turn slowly toward me," a gruff, whiskey tuned voice said. Nestor spun, pulling his weapon, and dove to the floor, firing twice on the way down. One other shot rang out and Nestor growled in pain as the bullet tore through arm. The gun fell from his hand at the shock of the wound, and he rolled twice when he hit the floor.

It was very quiet in the dark kitchen and Nestor, his wounded arm bleeding heavily, slowly got to his feet. He retrieved his weapon and saw the crumpled and dead body of an old man splayed out on the floor, a single shot flint-lock pistol still in his hand. "Just about got me old man. Don't know why people give warnings like that. Should have just shot me when I came through the door, stupid," he snarled.

His arm ached and blood was dripping onto the floor when he sat down at the small table to tend it. "That big old lead ball went right on through," he muttered and used some rags on the table to wrap the wound. "I gotta get that horse out of sight and see what kind of new home I have." He was chuckling at his good fortune walking out to the dilapidated shed.

CHAPTER NINETEEN

Washoe City had been the Washoe County Seat until the railroad through Reno populated that area and Reno replaced the lakeside community. The sheriff maintained a large staff in Washoe City and they were mobilizing following the wire from Ormsby County. Dirk Masterson came from San Francisco following the silver rush to the Comstock, didn't much care for working underground, and took up the tin badge.

Masterson, nearing fifty years, was resident deputy and had four men at his disposal in Washoe City. "Looks like this Nestor feller is coming our way. Cochran says he's a killer, so keep your eyes open. Here's a flyer with a good picture of the man. Let's spread out and find him.

"Any of you boys remember Terrence Corcoran?" Nobody answered. "He was with the Virginia City Sheriff's office a few years ago. He's Eureka County deputy now and is following Nestor. He's a wild one and almost as dangerous as Nestor. Try to remember he's on our side."

Masterson had to snicker remembering all the going's

on when Corcoran shot the sheriff. There were times he would have been willing to shoot his boss but never quite got around to it. "Sun'll be going down soon, so let's get this fool. Spread out and watch for anything unusual. Nestor might be trying to hole up." He knew he would be if he thought Corcoran was on his tail.

Masterson wore a Colt, had a rifle in his saddle scabbard, and grabbed a double barrel shotgun as he headed out the door. He rode out to the main road and turned south hoping to intercept either Nestor or Corcoran. Spring was slow coming on and as the sun slipped behind Slide Mountain the air took on a decided chill. Early spring in western Nevada could turn to winter within minutes.

The deputy saw smoke coming from homes and businesses and watched as many men were making their way home from work in the mills, iron shops, and businesses. A man on horseback would stand out this time of day. Men walked to work and back, didn't take horse or carriage, and Masterson spotted one rider coming toward him immediately.

"Hold up there, Corcoran. I've been looking for you," he bellowed.

"Well, my goodness, looky here. Dirk Masterson. I thought they would have put you out to pasture a few years ago. You look mighty fit, pard."

"You two, Irish. How close did you get to him?"

"I thought he was right in front of me, but some freighters got between us. I think he slipped off the trail. Gonna be dark shortly." Corcoran was looking all around hoping to pick up the trail. "He's the kind of fool who will bust in on a house full of people, Dirk."

"I know, I read the broadsheet. I've got three men roaming around and looking at the main road too. How did you get on his trail? I thought you were in Eureka?"

"It's one hell of a story, Dirk, and you need to know all about it."

"Let's ride over there to Charley Soo's place," Masterson said. "He makes strong coffee and always has a bottle of brandy tucked away behind the counter." While they made the ten-minute ride, Corcoran told him about Hog Mercer, Indians on the warpath, army intervention, women being killed, held captive, and violated, and why he was chasing Slim Nestor.

"And that's all there is to it?" Masterson laughed. "Good old Terrence Corcoran. You haven't changed one damn bit, old man. Do you really think the army will back down once they get on the march?"

"Not for one minute," Corcoran said. "Captain Hochstettler seems to be pretty sure, though. He's got a lot of backing from Major McPherson, and he's riding with Jaime Maldonado, who I trust all the way."

"Well, we better stop this Nestor feller so you can get back to your Indian war, old man," Masterson chuckled.

"Charley Soo is about sixty, a Chinese gentleman who worked on the railroad across the Sierra Nevada. He moved to Washoe City when the Chinese laborers were laid off and opened a diner. Corcoran, he makes the best Texas fried steak you've ever had."

As they rode near the diner Corcoran pointed out a single track leading up to a dark stone cabin. "Fresh prints, Dirk and no lights on. Half an hour later and we wouldn't have seen this.

"Anybody living in that cabin? Looks pretty run down even from this distance."

"A couple of old drunks. Wore-out and tired old miners. John Templeton was taken to the hospital a few days ago and his partner, Freddy Heinz should still be there."

"He's in trouble if these hoof prints carried Slim Nestor up there," Corcoran said.

"Stay on this, Corcoran. I'll go get us some backup. Good job, old man," he said turning his horse and loping off to find his deputies. Corcoran rode a little farther down the main highway and found some trees to hunker down by. He tied Rube off and made his way through heavy brush back toward the single-track pathway.

The big mountains to the west of Washoe Valley tower well over ten thousand feet and when the sun dips behind them, there isn't time for twilight. "I won't have to worry about bein' seen, anyway," Corcoran chuckled. "I might kill myself trippin' over something, though."

"I'm gonna need a fire but sure as hell I'm not lighting a lamp tonight," Nestor growled, surveying the kitchen. He had taken the body of the old man out and dumped it behind the shed and moved his horse into a stall in the shed. "That damned old man doesn't even have any decent food in this wreck of a cabin."

His arm throbbed and he was weak from loss of blood, but he was able to think and corrected himself right away about lighting a lamp. "The old man lives here, it's getting dark, and he would light the lamp." He cussed himself some finding lamps and getting them lit. "Need to find food."

He found a canister with less than two pounds of flour, a small bag of beans, and another canister with coffee. "Not even a damn bottle of whiskey." The cabinets didn't have doors so what was on the shelves was obvious, and there wasn't much. Nestor found two cots in a second room and ransacked that area coming up with one double eagle and two silver dollars.

"What a find," he sneered. Even so he pocketed the money. In the small front room Nestor found a bottle of whiskey about half full and took a big swallow. "That's better," he chuckled. When he tore the cushions from a large chair he had to catch his breath. "That's a bank bag if I've ever seen one. And it's heavy."

He had the canvas bag in one hand and the bottle in the other when he almost ran for the kitchen. "Got to light a fire. The old man would have, anyway. What was I thinking. Not seeing a light and smoke from the stove would be a give-away."

His fingers were almost twitching as he cut the top off the locked canvas bag and emptied it. More than fifty double eagles spilled onto the table along with several bundles of paper money. He looked at one of the bundles and wanted to howl to the moon. They were all hundred-dollar bills. There had to be ten thousand dollars in each bundle.

"That old man was a bank robber," Nestor laughed. "Drinkin' bad whiskey and living in a pig sty when he could have been eating oysters and drinkin' champagne in San Francisco. Well, he's dead and I'm not." He also knew he was close to being in real trouble. "I'm not trapped but I'm damn close to it. Go east and I'm in Virginia City with the sheriff waiting for me. Can't go west or back south.

"It's Reno or just stay in this miserable cabin and starve to death. Posse or no, I'm leaving out of here before sunrise." He stuffed up the old stove and got a pot of coffee boiling along with a pot of beans, and made plans for spending a lot of someone else's money.

"I should just hunker down and wait for Masterson but I gotta know what's going on in that cabin." Corcoran made his way through heavy brush and was within twenty or so feet from the back of the old shed. "Whoever is in there, the old man or Nestor, has a fire going and a lamp lit, but that just makes it more difficult to get close."

There was junk scattered all about, metal containers, harness, bottles, and baling wire everywhere, and Corcoran had to move slow and easy. "I'm gonna kill myself sure as hell," he chuckled. "What's this?" He stood back from something soft he tripped over. He knelt down and felt about. His hands came up bloody and he knew whoever lit the fire and lamps, wasn't the old man.

He moved as slowly as possible into the shed and found Nestor's horse munching some hay. "That's Hatch's horse he stole." Corcoran spoke quietly to the horse as he untied him and led him out the back of the shed and down the pathway to the main road. "There are times I like the dark of night. This'll slow Mr. Nestor down some."

As he tied off Hatch's horse next to Rube, Masterson rode up with two deputies. "Whatcha got there, Corcoran?"

"I do believe this is what Nestor rode in on, Dirk.

Found the body of an old man behind a shed up there. Whoever's in the cabin has lit a fire and has a lamp burning. I didn't try to get too close."

"Good. We'll surround the cabin and call that fool out," Masterson said. "You want the front, Terrence?"

"Always," Corcoran laughed.

CHAPTER TWENTY

"Any word from Corcoran?" Major McPherson stuck his head in Syd Cochran's office.

"Not a word, Major. How about you? Anything from Fort McDermitt?"

"Only that my volunteers have hooked up with Hochstettler and Knightbridge. The war never happened, thank God. I may have an intra-military war on my hands, however. How about Hatch? Is he gonna live?"

"Long enough to stand trial," Cochran laughed. "The knife cut deep but didn't kill him. There will be others implicated by those papers Corcoran found. That was a big organization Hatch put together. You gonna win your war?"

"Hatch's operation could have gone for a long time if Hog Mercer hadn't kidnapped that little girl. I'm going to win, you can bet your new silver spurs on that. What's your next move, Sheriff?"

"I'm meeting with the U.S. Attorney General this morning. It's all in his lap after that. There were many local laws broken but not many in my county. At least one feedlot operator will be out of business and there will probably be changes to branding and land law in the next legislature. You?"

"I'm riding north to lead the detachment back to Fort McDermitt. I need to have a serious talk with a young lieutenant and the post commander up there. I'll be riding as a full colonel. Just got the confirmation. If you do hear from Corcoran, tell him I'd like to have him with me." McPherson liked the way Corcoran saw through problems with the least emotion. "I'd love to have five officers like him working for me."

"You'd court martial him within a week, Major," Syd Cochran laughed.

"I wish we had two more people, Corcoran. As dark as it is, we better not be shooting each other." Dirk Masterson wanted to put one man on each of two sides of the cabin. That way he would take one, and Corcoran would come from the side of the building where the lamp shown through a window. "At least he can't hightail it out on a horse."

"Sure would like to do this about three in the morning, but we shouldn't wait. Got a plan?" Corcoran was going to follow protocol, at least try to. "It is your jurisdiction."

Masterson almost laughed at the comment. "I do, but tell me yours," he chuckled.

"When I call him out and mention that he's surrounded, each of you in turn yell out, so he knows that he is surrounded. I'd rather not kill the fool if we don't have to. He knows the whole story and I'm sure the feds will want him."

"Good," Dirk Masterson said. "Let's get in position, boys. Give us ten minutes, Corcoran, then make your play. Nice and quiet now," he said, disappearing in the night shadows.

Corcoran eased through the brush and was able to get within twenty feet of the kitchen door, but there wasn't anything closer that he could hide behind. There was a broken down carriage off to his left that would have put him within ten feet of that door but the run to it was wide open to anyone looking out that window. He decided to take that chance, held his breath, and slowly crept across the open space, low to the ground. He hid in the shadows of the carriage to wait for the others to get as close as possible. Hard as he looked he couldn't see any movement inside.

It was a long ten minutes and he finally cupped his hands and yelled at the cabin. "Hello the house, This is Deputy Sheriff Corcoran. Throw out your weapons and step out of the cabin." He waited for only a minute before hollering again.

"You are surrounded. Give yourself up and you will live. Again, throw out your weapons and step out of the cabin. You are surrounded."

One at a time Masterson and his deputies hollered out where they were and Corcoran figured he would only give Nestor another minute to make his move. It came sooner than that. The lamp was doused and the kitchen window shattered before two quick shots were fired. Corcoran fired two back, aiming for where he saw that gun barrel spitting fire.

Masterson yelled out for his men to stay where they were. He moved toward the porch at the front of the house, almost crawling through heavy brush. Corcoran ran from behind the carriage to the side of the house, near that broken window. He was about to move under the window and toward the door when he again saw the barrel of a revolver. He tried to judge where the person holding that gun would be, aimed, and fired.

The continued howling told him he scored, but didn't kill the man. "He's hit Masterson but I can't tell if he's out of the fight yet."

"Keep him busy, Corcoran," Masterson yelled back and moved up onto the porch. He crawled to the door, found it unlocked, and from the side slowly opened it. There was no reaction to that and he crawled through the door and into the dark room.

"I'm coming for you, Nestor," Corcoran yelled. "There's fifteen of us out here ready to kill your filthy butt. Throw your weapon out and you might not die tonight." He reached up and opened the door, keeping as far to the side as possible.

He heard Nestor groan and knew the man was trying to hide behind something. Corcoran groped around the dirt where he was spread out and found a rock, which he tossed through the door. Two quick shots rang out and then a third from the front room.

Nestor screamed and Corcoran heard the pistol fall to the floor. "Coming in," he yelled racing through the door. He found Nestor thrashing about, howling in pain, and bleeding heavily from two wounds. One shot had blown through an upper arm, smashing bone and muscle, and a second was a belly shot, which bled profusely.

"Run for the doc," Masterson yelled at one of his deputies as Corcoran got the lamp lit. Nestor was in horrible pain and it took Corcoran several minutes to get the bleeding in his arm stopped.

"Not sure we can do anything about the stomach wound, Nestor. Too dumb to know you were whipped, eh? Well, if you live through this you've got the gallows and a long rope to think about." Corcoran ripped Nestor's shirt aside and wadded up a rag from the table to place over the wound.

"You gotta see this, Corcoran. Look what the man had with him." The contents of the canvas bank bag were still spread out on the table. "There must be sixty or seventy thousand dollars here. My God, Corcoran, look."

"Hatch and them made good money on their cattle scheme but not that good," Corcoran said. "That has to be from a bank job, Masterson. Any big robberies around here lately?"

"Nothing that big," Masterson chuckled. "This bag is from a bank in New Mexico Territory. Nestor from around there?"

"He's been in this country for at least three years according to Hatch's records. You don't suppose one of the drunks that lived here was a bank robber do you?"

They were still laughing when Doctor Durdin walked in. "A wounded man is nothing to laugh at, gentlemen." He knelt down to look at Nestor. "He needs to be moved to a bed and quickly."

Two deputies grabbed Nestor and carried him to one of the cots and laid him out. "I'd like him to make trial so we can hang the bastard, Doc," Corcoran snarled. "I don't laugh at criminals, only at fools." The big man towered over the diminutive doctor who simply snuffed some and followed the wounded man into the bedroom.

"Easy, Terrence, old friend. Doc Durdin is a grouch all the time but he does tend to save more lives than he loses. I'm going to leave a deputy here with the doc until we can move Nestor into a cell. I gotta get this money into a safe and follow up on where it might have come from. I'll scare the hell out of Templeton when I walk up to his hospital bed and challenge him on why they had all this money in the cabin." He chuckled some and rustled several bundles of hundred dollar bills about on the table.

"It looks a lot like your job is about over, sir. No more Indian war, no little girls to save, and no more cattle being stole. Not bad for a man on vacation," Masterson laughed.

"There's one little job left to do. I have to find Sarah Sonnett and say goodbye to the fine lady. And then again, I might not be able to say goodbye." The vision of that ranch out there in Dixie Valley still looked mighty good. Was it good enough to make the lawman put aside that little tin badge?

He knew it wasn't, knew he and Sarah Sonnett would never be a couple, and knew that he needed to get back to the peace and quiet of Eureka County. "I'm riding back to Carson City and head for home with a couple of stops along the way. I've still got gear spread out all across the state."

"So, you got your man, eh? I'm glad," Ormsby County Sheriff Sydney Cochran said. He was sitting behind his big desk, coffee in one hand and a flask of brandy in the other. "Care for a pick-me-up?"

"I would, indeed," Corcoran said. He neglected to put any coffee in his cup, just filled it up with decent brandy. "I doubt that Nestor will live to face trial, Syd. He was shot right in the middle of his belly and that usually means death. Did that wire you're shaking in my face say anything about a bunch of money?"

"Seventy eight thousand dollars and change, Terrence. Came from a bank job in Santa Fe five years ago. Those two men were just sitting on it. In five years they managed to spend less than two thousand dollars from their take."

"My, but I do love stupid criminals. Well, keep in touch, I'm heading home," Corcoran said.

"Nope, afraid you're not. Here's a note from McPherson. Wants you to catch up to him on the trail to Fort McDermitt. Maybe you could ride through Virginia City and say hello to some of your friends."

"I'd never catch up to McPherson if I did," Corcoran laughed. "Well, damn," he said, reading the note. "Guess I'm not going home yet."

CHAPTER TWENTY-ONE

It's a long haul from Carson City to Fort McDermitt and Corcoran didn't know exactly where he would meet up with McPherson and his combined force. Spring was more evident, at least, and he made good time getting to the Black Rock Desert but he did make a wide arc around the Paiute village at Pyramid Lake. "Our war might be over but some of those boys still might want some of my delightful hair," he chuckled. Once on the Black Rock playa he had no trouble locating the army's trail across that big flat plain.

"You had a good jump on me Major but I'm riding a whole lot faster than you," he laughed putting Rube in a strong trot. There was no wind, the temperature was a comfortable seventy-six or so, and he intercepted the large army force along the Quinn River where it was encamped for the night.

"Halt and be recognized," the voice came out of the twilight.

"Name's Corcoran, Terrence Corcoran. Major McPherson is expecting me."

"Advance and be recognized," the private said. Corcoran eased into his light. "Nice to see you again. Wait here with me and I'll send for a guide. The colonel's been thinking you'd show up tomorrow."

There were well over two hundred people in the camp and a private who insisted on saluting Corcoran led him to McPherson. "That man salutes me one more time and I'm gonna break his arm," Corcoran snarled as Corporal Leon Smith showed him to the command tent. Smith had a hard time choking off his chuckles and got a severe glare from First Sergeant Ramsay.

A long table was set up at a fire outside the tent and supper was about to be served. Several men were roasting half a deer and there were several flasks set about too. "My timing was right," he quipped walking up to McPherson, resplendent in his new Colonel's uniform.

Between platters of roasted venison, bowls of soup, and cups of whiskey, Corcoran brought everyone up to speed. "Hatch will live to stand trial but Slim Nestor might not. I don't know how we managed to keep this under control, McPherson, but it looks like Paiute War Number Three ain't gonna be in the history books."

He noticed that the feisty Lieutenant Knightbridge was glaring at him, angry, wanted to say something, and knew he would suffer greatly if he did. "That bothers you, doesn't it Knightbridge," Corcoran said. "You believe that old adage, the only good Indian is a dead Indian. That hate could ruin your life."

"Men like you who meddle in army business tend to make my life difficult," he responded.

"That's enough, Lieutenant," McPherson snapped.

"It's quite all right, Colonel," Corcoran said. "For your information, Knightbridge, dealing with Indian problems is not just army business. The government has created the Bureau of Indian Affairs to supplant the army. Some in that agency, like our Mr. Hatch, use their position for personal benefit, and that, too, isn't army business."

Corcoran looked over at Jaime Maldonado for confirmation and the Indian lawman smiled before commenting. "The army is changing its ways with the tribes, too, Lieutenant. Wanton killing is not how people get along," he said. "There were many wrongs that brought this episode with the Paiute tribe to a head. Many committed by white men, several committed by Indians, and your approach to the problem would have blown the entire thing out of all proportion.

"Listen to what the colonel has been saying and when we get to Fort McDermitt and all the reports are written, take the time to read and understand just what did happen."

Knightbridge was not a stupid man, but his hatred of Indians was deep. "I'm just as American as you are, Lieutenant," Maldonado continued. "I was born in California the year after it became part of the United States. Our family lived in the Santa Barbara area for more than one hundred years, first under Spanish rule, then Mexican, and now, American. And with that said, you still have a hatred of Mexicans, Indians, and everyone else that isn't white."

"Periods of introspection might help, sir. You're an intelligent man with a good career in front of you. It's time to put your hatred aside."

Knightbridge wanted to jump up, swipe everything off

that long table and kill Maldonado and Corcoran, run his sabre through Colonel McPherson, and rip his uniform to shreds. But, he was a commissioned officer in the United States Army, an officer and a gentleman, and despite the sting from the Indian lawman's words, he sat still.

Was this dark skinned man right? Did he really hate everyone who was not white? Was he going to kill those Indians for a reason? Or from hatred? Knightbridge sat very quiet, first just staring at his empty plate, then making eye contact with everyone at the table. His first reaction was to resent what Maldonado and Corcoran said, but he also had too many highly personal questions that had to be answered.

"May I be excused, Colonel?"

"I think that's best. We'll talk in the morning, Lieutenant."

Knightbridge stood, nodded to those at the table, and left with a straight back and squared shoulders. "He has the makings of a fine officer if he can control that hate," Colonel McPherson said.

"What exactly am I riding into, joining up with you, Colonel?" Corcoran couldn't understand just why he should even be at that table. He was a civilian, a deputy sheriff well out of his jurisdiction, riding to Fort McDermitt with a large detachment of the army. "I can't for the life of me understand why I'm here."

"We'll talk about that in the morning, Corcoran. Get a good night's sleep. We've a long ride tomorrow."

He had been assigned a tent in officer's country and walked slowly toward it, passing Knightbridges' quarters. The lieutenant stepped out of the shadows and hailed

Corcoran. "If we ever meet in neutral territory, Corcoran, I'll kill you on sight."

"We could take a little walk into the darkness of the desert right now, Knightbridge, if you feel up to it. McPherson sees a lot in you that I sure can't fathom. Minutes ago he called you a fine officer. I'm calling you a stupid man filled with hate. I've spent most of my life dealing with stupid men, some are in prison, many are dead."

"If you want some of my hide, mister, make your move now or shut your stupid mouth and walk away."

Knightbridge stood rock still. He hadn't been spoken to like that since he was a little boy. Anger, white hot, flowed through him, blurring his vision, his hands were shaking, not from fear, but from that anger. At the last second, just as Corcoran was ready for a fist, a gun, or a saber, Knightbridge turned and stormed into his tent.

Knightbridge was raised in a moneyed east coast family and carried a heavy coat of arrogance that was unfortunately fine tuned at the Military Academy. He took umbrage at slightest comment or phrase, seldom walked from an encounter, and felt that Corcoran was nothing but a backwoods bumpkin with a tin star from a neglected county in a second rate state.

Corcoran grabbed his blanket off the cot and walked to where Rube was being held, untied the big gelding and walked into the desert half a mile. "I think I'll sleep under the stars tonight, old man," he chuckled, laying the blanket out. "That young man might choke on his own bile before morning."

. . .

"We'll be getting underway in about an hour, Mr. Corcoran. The Colonel asks that you join him at his table." The young private found Corcoran preparing his pack for the long trip home. The private saluted about three times and came close to a broken jaw before he lit out. Corcoran was up well before the sun and back in his tent when the orderly arrived.

"Don't ever do that again," Corcoran snarled. He couldn't tell you why he hated the concept of someone saluting another, but a look at his history would certainly tell you. Corcoran was a born leader yet fought against taking the lead position. He would rather be a deputy than sheriff, would rather have someone with him, such as Pappy Somerset, than lead a group, even though everyone in the group looked to him as their leader.

Corcoran never gave it a thought about why people wanted to ride with him, wanted to stand with him in a big fight, wanted to learn from him, and he did everything he could to never assume a position of leadership. "All men are good at what they do best," he said once, "and no man should be forced to salute another unless he meant it."

Colonel McPherson had several people at the table, Knightbridge, Hochstettler, and Maldonado among them. "Morning, Corcoran. We'll be at McDermitt this afternoon," he said. He looked around the table, waiting for Corcoran to get seated. Corcoran muttered a good morning, glanced at Knightbridge and got a glare back.

"Lieutenant Knightbridge, I want you to form a detail and ride ahead to inform Captain Caldwell of our approach. I'll write a dispatch for you to carry to the post commander."

"Yes sir," Knightbridge said. He stood and glared again at Corcoran who helped matters along by smiling broadly at the man. Knightbridge stormed off to form his detail.

"Captain Hochstettler, you're in command. I'm just along for the ride. Bring us in smartly."

Hochstettler smiled and nodded, but McPherson wasn't quite finished. "Please stand, Hochstettler. You might find these a bit more comfortable to wear," and he handed a jewelry box to him. Hochstettler opened it to find the oak leaves of a major inside. "They aren't quite as heavy as captain's bars."

Hurrahs and clapping echoed about and Hochstettler offered a smart salute to the colonel. "I'm humbled, sir," is all he said.

"This episode with Hatch and company has shown in blatant colors what happens when there is no law presence in a large area. From Dayton east to Austin, a great swath of central Nevada, there is no law and Mercer, Whitney, and Watson took advantage of that. I spoke with the governor before leaving Carson City, Corcoran, and suggested that a ranger or marshal should be appointed to bring law and order to the area.

"I didn't do that as Nevada's highest ranking military officer, I did it as a citizen. It isn't a military problem so I really have no jurisdiction. However, after hearing what had happened and what had almost happened, the governor was very open to my suggestion."

Before McPherson could go any further Corcoran spoke up. "If you're suggesting that I take such a position, the answer is no, Colonel. I have a fine job in Eureka County."

"No, Corcoran, although you would be a fine choice, what I wanted to ask you is, will you give the governor a few suggestions on who might make a fine marshal for that area."

"When the stink clears from the Indian Agency's offices in Carson City, I rather doubt that Jaime Maldonado would want to stay. He knows central Nevada like no one else. That's the only name I'd offer. You can wire that to the governor when you reach McDermitt, in my name if you wish. I just want to get home."

"What are your thoughts on that Maldonado?" McPherson hoped that Corcoran would suggest the Indian lawman.

"I think the bureau will be in an uproar for some time when the Hatch thing goes public. They certainly won't want to take responsibility for any of it. I would be honored to accept such a position. I have many friends throughout that region, many have complained about the lack of law, and would support my efforts to clean up the territory."

"Will the agency try to implicate you, Jaime?" Corcoran had been worried about that from the beginning. He had his own questions about where Maldonado stood when he first heard about the cattle rustling and sales. "Hatch was their chosen man, after all. They might be looking for a scapegoat."

"They might at that, Corcoran," Maldonado smiled. He pulled a cheroot out of his pocket and lit it, letting the sweet smoke filter through his nose. "But I've kept meticulous records of my own, and with the papers you filched from Hatch, nothing they say can implicate me," he chuckled.

"Then consider yourself the Lahontan Valley Marshal, sir." Colonel McPherson lit his own cigar and poured some brandy into his morning coffee. "There is no doubt the governor will consent."

"There's a lot more to it than that, Colonel. The logistics of creating such an office should be spelled out and done by way of a governing body." Maldonado was thinking about deputies, offices, jails, and of course, paychecks.

"I'm sure the governor will take care of all that. Consider it done," McPherson said. The idea of small-minded politicians getting in the way never entered the colonel's mind and Maldonado was quite willing to ride with whatever happened as long as he was no longer associated with the Indian agency.

"Good," Corcoran said. "I'm gone." He strode from the gathering, packed what little he had with him, gathered up pack mule, and rode out of camp in less than half an hour. "First, East Gate Station, Rube, then it's Eureka and my own bed."

There was no road or trail that led from where he was to the western front of the Desatoya Range, and Corcoran simply rode off cross country. The desert gave way to sage and brush covered rangeland, rocky and filled with protruding hills and deep arroyos. He was climbing a long hill when he noticed Rube twitching his ears back and forth. "What is it, old man?" He turned in the saddle and gave that horse a solid kick in the ribs. "Let's ride, boy."

The dust plume was at least a mile behind him and Corcoran pushed hard for a stand of rocks and cedar brush a hundred yards or so to his west. He got into the copse of brush and got the animals tied off as quickly as he could wondering who would be on his trail. "I sure wasn't working to hide my trail," he murmured in disgust getting his extension glass out.

He hunkered down in the brush, his rifle at the ready, trying to get a good view of the single rider coming along at a gentle trot. "That's an army rig and the man's in an officer's uniform. Come on, man, lift your head a bit," he snarled. It was several minutes before Corcoran was able to identify Lieutenant Knightbridge as the rider following his trail.

"He's supposed to be leading a detachment to Fort McDermitt not trailing me. Damn fool is what he is. Wonder what Pappy would say about this young lieutenant?" He had to chuckle watching Knightbridge pick up where Corcoran made his run for the rocks. "You get your little butt a bit closer and there's a surprise awaiting, son," he whispered, leveling the Winchester.

"That's about far enough, Knightbridge," Corcoran hollered, and fired a shot into the dirt in front of his horse. "I ain't in the mood for stupid. Get on out of here while you can."

Knightbridge grabbed his rifle and dove off the horse, He scrambled into some brush along a narrow gulch and Corcoran heard him lever a round in the rifle. "This isn't gonna be the end of your career, Knightbridge, it's gonna be the end of your life. Now think about that."

The answer came from a bullet ricocheting off the rocks about ten feet from Corcoran. "So, he doesn't know where I am, eh?" Corcoran muttered. "No more talk, now. Let's see what this fool has."

Knightbridge was in an awkward position and knew it. He let himself down into the shallow depression and squirmed along until he was able to come back up under a stand of cedar brush. He knew Corcoran was somewhere in those rocks above him but couldn't pinpoint the man. This was when he needed a couple of troopers to move about and force Corcoran to show himself.

There was a stand of rocks about twenty feet up and in front of him and if he could get to them he would be in a much better position. He jumped to his feet and started the dash across the open plain and Corcoran spotted the movement immediately. One shot rang out and Knightbridge went down in a heap, his right leg ripped open at the knee.

"I could just ride off and let you bleed to death, Lieutenant," Corcoran hollered down to the man. "On the other hand you could throw your guns out and I could try to save your worthless life. What'll it be?"

What the hell's the matter with stupid people? Corcoran was thinking. *He's washing away everything he's worked for his whole life. Because I shamed him? Stupid, stupid, stupid.* "I ain't gonna move on you, Lieutenant. Just gonna sit here with a canteen full of cool water and wait for you to die so I can go on home."

He watched Knightbridge crawl into the stand of rock, leaving a definite trail of blood. "I ain't gonna shoot again, Knightbridge. I'm just gonna wait until you're dead and ride off home." He was answered by another rifle shot that wasn't within fifteen feet of where he stood. "Nice shootin', Lieutenant. Busted that rock clean as all get out. How's your leg feel?"

"I'll get you, Corcoran. I'll kill you," Knightbridge yelled.

"Big talk for a wounded man without backup. I'm

looking down at your horse, Lieutenant. You left your canteen. Not smart, old man. I can still save your stinkin' butt. All you got to do is throw those weapons out. You're runnin' out of time and you know it." He picked up a rock and threw it into the brush off to his right and Knightbridge immediately took a shot where it clattered about.

"You are frightfully stupid, mister. Give it up," Corcoran laughed out.

The pain from the shattered knee was getting worse, shock was setting in, and loss of blood was making Knightbridge weak. He could feel the fingers of death tightening their hold and made one desperate move toward his horse. He crawled about fifteen feet when Corcoran jumped on his back and bashed him in the head with his rifle.

Corcoran dragged the army officer to his horse, tied the horse off and brought his own animals down and got them settled. He lit a fire and was working to clean the knee wound when the lieutenant regained consciousness. "You bastard," Knightbridge said and made a move for his sidearm, which he discovered wasn't there.

"Be nice, stupid." Corcoran slapped him across the side of the head and continued work on his wound. He had it cleaned and wrapped with a pant leg from the soldier when he saw more dust on his back trail. "Looks like the entire brigade is looking for you, Knightbridge. You might live after all. 'Course you won't be wearing all that gold and braid and stuff. Won't be no privates runnin' around salutin' you every ten feet."

"You won't have the benefit of a first sergeant like old Michael Ramsay to see to it that things are done right.

Nope, you'll just be another stupid ex soldier lookin' for a job. That is, if you live." Corcoran dumped some brandy on the open wound to make his point and laughed at the screaming that followed. "Yup, old man, I am one mean sumbitch when I want to be."

CHAPTER TWENTY-TWO

"How did you know to get on his trail?" Corcoran was sitting at the fire with Major Hochstettler and First Sergeant Ramsay, enjoying a cup of coffee laced with the colonel's brandy.

"Ramsay was putting the detail together for the ride to Fort McDermitt and couldn't find the lieutenant. It didn't take a great mind to figure out what was going on. A search of his tent and we knew he had deserted. We didn't know that he was following you until we were well on his trail."

"We fully expected to come across his body," Ramsay said with a slight chuckle that drew a frown from Major Hochstettler.

"Colonel McPherson is taking the command on in and I was dispatched to save you, Corcoran," he laughed. "Save you, we did, eh Sergeant?"

"Indeed, sir," Ramsay laughed right out, this time. "Between us, Corcoran, he would have been better off if you had killed him."

"Probably true, Ramsay. He'll face a court martial and years in prison or, more likely, a quick hanging. For sure, that leg can't be saved. Hate is a terrible thing, Sergeant. You fight enemies of the nation, I fight criminals, and we both detest those we fight because of what they do or represent. He fought because he hated who they were. It's a fine line, but it is there."

"I'm sure the colonel would want you to help us escort this man back to the fort, Corcoran," Hochstettler said. "You'll need to testify and make your reports."

"I'm going to disappoint the colonel, I'm afraid," Corcoran chuckled. "I'll write your report, in detail, but you won't need my testimony. His actions alone will get him hung. No, Fort McDermitt is that way," he pointed off to the northeast, "and home is that way," he said. "I will take some more of your brandy, though," he laughed, filling his cup.

Fires were lit and the troopers settled in for their dinner with guards posted and orders given. "I'll be off in the morning, Major. It's hard to remember that I was simply going to take a couple of weeks off and visit some old friends. I can just imagine what the sheriff is saying about now."

"When I think how close we came to a full blown war with the Paiutes I have to shudder just a bit," Hochstettler said. "Sure, we would have whipped their butts good, killed many men, women, and children, and then found out there was no reason to. Good men are good regardless of color or background, Corcoran."

"Yes, and bad men are bad, also regardless. Just one lawman operating in the Lahontan Valley would have prevented all of this. The Mercer boys would have been taken in for rustling and that first girl wouldn't have died. The Whitney family would have been in jail.

"I hope everything falls into place for Jaime Maldonado. He's a good man." Corcoran sat back in a camp chair, hot coffee and brandy working their magic on his tired and aching body. He finally let his body take control. "Give the colonel my regards and I'll be off before first light," and made his way to his bedroll.

Corcoran rode south without benefit of trails, his mule filled with supplies from the army and it was a long uneventful three days later, along the west flanks of the Desatoya Range that he pulled Rube to a stop at the East Gate Station. One of the horse boys ran out to welcome him.

"Mr. Carothers sure will be glad to see you," he said. "I'll take care of everything for you."

"Thanks Cory. Any problems while I was gone?"

"Not from the Indians," he said, taking the lead rope from Corcoran and leading the two animals toward the barns.

Corcoran walked toward the big rambling ranch house wondering what that comment might have meant. There were several horses tied off at the hitching rails and he noticed that the corrals were filled with horses. "The stages must be running again. Hope everyone was safe."

Ralph Carothers was sitting in front of the fire when Corcoran came in and jumped to his feet. "Where the hell you been, Corcoran? Been worried sick you got yourself all killed or something horrible like that."

Corcoran was laughing and hugged his old friend.

"Been a little busy fighting off Indians, Indian agents, and other vermin, Ralph. How's Sarah Sonnett? Did Reb recover? Did Pappy Somerset get to you in time? What about that young Abe Johnson? He okay?"

Corcoran was about to ask even more questions when Sarah walked into the large great room. "Terrence, you're back." She rushed across the room and wrapped her arms around him. "We were all worried." She stood back some and gave him a full appraisal. "You look just fine, Terrence."

"So, Corcoran," Carothers said, "tell us your story and we'll tell you ours." They settled into the large chairs set about in front of the massive stone fireplace and Corcoran spent the next twenty minutes or so telling about the downfall of Hatch and company.

"It came that close to the army attacking the Paiute village?" Sarah asked. "What a horrible thing that would have been. Jaime is going to be the Lahontan Valley Marshal? That's wonderful news, but all the known criminals are dead," she laughed.

"That's the problem with criminals," Corcoran chuckled. "There's always a new crop coming up. I'm sure Maldonado will find himself with plenty of work." He drank some of the brandy that had been offered around. "Now, it's your turn. Tell me your story, Mrs. Sonnett."

"Well, that's part of the story, Terrence," Ralph Carothers said. He got up from his big chair and walked to Sarah's and sat next to her. "This lovely lady is now known as Mrs. Ralph Carothers."

"Isn't it wonderful, Terrence?" Her eyes were dancing with warmth and she took Carothers' hand and held it to her. "We spent three days in that cold miserable camp near the big sand dunes nursing Reb. Abe Johnson shot another deer so we had plenty of food and he left to take care of his ranch."

"So, I turn my back for just a minute and the idea of fighting off Indian marauders and keeping everyone safe turns into a love fest?" Corcoran was laughing and had to fill his tumbler with brandy again.

"Ralph was worn out nurse-maiding me and Reb, and, well, all of nature came together. We're going to make this into a fine cattle ranch again when the stage line moves their station to Cold Springs Canyon. We'll move cattle and sheep between here and Dixie Valley, and use some of the high elevation areas in the Desatoya Mountains for summer pasture."

"Yup, Reb will be at the Dixie Valley ranch and we'll be here. I think the news about Maldonado is the best of all. With a real lawman in the valley, and so much good land available, people should be able to move back in and feel safe." Ralph Carothers sat back in the comfortable sofa and looked happier than Corcoran had seen him in years.

"I think that's wonderful," Corcoran said. He looked at the two of them and knew that Ralph would again be the strong happy man he had been. "Stage station operator wasn't your calling, Ralph. This is absolutely for the best.

"I'll be leaving in the morning. Probably swing through the Monitor Valley and find old Pappy. Spent so much time fighting and chasing Indians we never did get a chance to talk long and hard. I hope you two have the best lives any two could have."

"I'll have supper ready in an hour or so, Terrence. Time for you to get yourself cleaned up a bit. You got a load of trail dust hovering about."

"Does that mean Miss Sadie is no longer on duty?"

"Miss Sadie is taking on the cook duties at the new Cold Springs Station and left here in a huff, Corcoran. She'll do fine up there," Carothers said.

Corcoran had to chuckle. "Maybe I understand what that boy in the barn meant. I asked if there had been any trouble and he said, 'not from the Indians.' She caused a ruckus, did she?"

"You might put it that way," Sarah said. "We have new crockery ordered. It's coming in from San Francisco and Ralph got the doors re-hung. We'll just board up the one window," she laughed. Ralph sat quietly, shaking his shaggy old head but with a smile on his face.

"What about the Watson girl? The last time I saw her she was a mess. Ma Hennessy was having trouble with her. She will have mental problems for a long time, I think."

"There were relatives back east, I guess," Sarah said. "The best thing to come out of all of this is that Tommy Hennessy is going to come to the Dixie Valley place and work for Reb. They have become like brothers and that boy became a man through all of this."

"No, Sarah, the best thing to come out of all of this is what I'm looking at right now. The two of you, sitting holding hands, operators of a beautiful cattle ranch."

A LOOK AT TOUGH WOMAN RANCH

(Terrence Corcoran book 5) by Johnny Gunn

CORCORAN IS ON THE CHASE...

A bank robbery prompts a chase by a posse to an outlaw hideout. Followed by a shootout at the hideout that leaves one outlaw and one deputy sheriff dead. The outlaws make for a far destination which brings Terrence Corcoran on the chase.

Deputies from three counties chase Brad Doolin across the wilderness of frontier Nevada. Doolin attempts to hole up at a ranch, kills the rancher, and in a wild fight, is captured.

A high excitement, action-filled western adventure from Johnny Gunn.

AVAILABLE MAY 2019

ABOUT THE AUTHOR

Reno, Nevada novelist, Johnny Gunn, is retired from a long career in journalism. He has worked in print, broadcast, and Internet, including a stint as publisher and editor of the Virginia City Legend. These days, Gunn spends most of his time writing novel length fiction, concentrating on the western genre. Or, you can find him down by the Truckee River with a fly rod in hand.

"it's been a wonderful life. I was born in Santa Cruz, California, on the north shore of fabled Monterey Bay. When I was fourteen, that would have been 1953, we moved to Guam and I went through my high school years living in a tropical paradise. I learned to scuba dive from a WWII Navy Frogman, learned to fly from a WWII combat pilot (by dad), but I knew how to fish long before I moved to Guam.

"I spent time on the Island of Truk, which during WWII was a huge Japanese naval base, and dived in the lagoon. Massive U.S. air strikes sunk thousands of tons of Japanese naval craft, and it was more than exciting to dive on those wrecks. In the Palau Islands, near Koror, I also dived on Japanese aircraft that had been shot down into the lagoons.

Made in the USA
Las Vegas, NV
25 March 2023

69656409R00146